# MORTAL BROTHER

## AN UNBOUNDED NOVELLA

# Books by Teyla Branton

**Unbounded Novels**
The Change
The Cure
The Escape
The Reckoning

**Unbounded Novellas**
Ava's Revenge
Mortal Brother
Lethal Engagement

**Under the Name Rachel Branton**
House Without Lies
Tell Me No Lies
Your Eyes Don't Lie
Royal Quest

# MORTAL BROTHER

AN UNBOUNDED NOVELLA

# TEYLA BRANTON

WHITE
STAR PRESS

This is a work of fiction, and the views expressed herein are the sole responsibility of the author. Likewise, certain characters, places, and incidents are the product of the author's imagination, and any resemblance to actual persons, living or dead, or actual events or locales, is entirely coincidental.

Mortal Brother (An Unbounded Novella)

Published by White Star Press
P.O. Box 353
American Fork, Utah 84003

Printed in the United States of America
ISBN: 978-1-939203-56-4
Year of first printing: 2015

To all my mortal readers, who wish secretly to be Unbounded. We can still be Renegades!

# CHAPTER 1

THE ARMED MEN CRAWLING ALL OVER MY PLANE WERE THE first indication that something wasn't right. Well, it wasn't exactly my plane, but I was a Renegade, and it belonged to our group, even if I was mortal and wouldn't live two thousand years like my Unbounded comrades. Besides, I was the only one who could fly the plane, so I considered it mine.

I'd thought taking care of the plane in this little out-of-the-way airstrip in the Mexican jungle while my friends looked into an attack on the medical lab we funded here was little more than babysitting duty, something to keep me away from the real action. Safe. More than a bit irritating, but if staying behind meant staying alive, I'd deal with the irritation for my two children, who had been through more than any children should since their mother's murder two months earlier.

I'd nearly lost them, too, yesterday when the Emporium had attacked our stronghold in Oregon. One of our men *had* died, so being safe wasn't all that bad.

Except now I'd bet the men trying to get inside that plane weren't doing it for my welfare.

"More coffee?" asked Diego Molina, the young Mexican who, along with his father, ran the airstrip. He put his hand on the pot of bad coffee sitting on the small table between us—the third pot since my arrival several hours ago. The coffee and the stale biscuits made me wonder if they were trying to poison me or simply weren't used to entertaining. If it hadn't been for the delicious smells coming from the attached kitchen and a promised dinner, I would have already retreated to the privacy—and comfort—of the plane.

"He is probably sick of that swill," a young woman said, appearing from the kitchen for the first time. She set a sweating can of beer in front of me and smiled. It was the first I'd seen of anyone besides the two men since my arrival. She wore tight, American-style jeans and a light blue tank top that hugged her small curves. She looked barely out of her teens and pretty in a dark, exotic way, with long black hair and eyes that were almost too large in her narrow face.

Ignoring the can, I jumped to my feet and strode to the small open window, stopping to draw out a pair of binoculars from my backpack of survival gear so I could see better. Across the wide expanse of dirt that sepa-rated this small building from where my plane sat, the strangers were inspecting the underbelly of the plane, presumably trying to find another way inside besides the locked door. That wasn't happening any time soon. Only our Renegades knew the combination to the hatches, and there was a handprint reader for added security. While they could eventually break the codes or drill through the mechanism, it would take time.

"What are they doing to my plane?" My hand went to my pistol, which suddenly seemed inadequate protection against the half dozen men. Rough men, who looked prepared to do whatever it took to achieve their goal, if the rifles slung over their shoulders were any indication.

Diego followed me to the window, his Adam's apple bobbing as he swallowed nervously. "I don't know," he said, his accent thicker than ever. Turning, he rattled off something in quick Spanish to his father, César, who still sat at the table.

The two men exchanged more rapid conversation, and then the older man stood and clumped to the outer door, pulling it open. A short time later, he was in the sedan he'd picked me up in and was speeding toward the plane. The men stopped banging on the lower hatch when they saw him coming. They clustered as they waited, and I thought it a promising sign when none of them attacked him as he climbed from the car.

The goodwill didn't last. We were too far away to hear anything said, but the violent gesturing told me the newcomers were angry. The pistol one of them waved around also spoke loudly of their intentions. Diego's father nodded and lifted his hands in an obvious plea for them to wait. Then he returned to his car and drove back across the dirt.

When César arrived, his wide, sun-darkened face was even darker with anger as he exchanged more words with his son. Diego looked the picture of a wounded child who had done something he knew he shouldn't have.

The girl's head yanked back and forth between them as she followed the conversation, the flush rising on her face making her more compelling. She spoke to the men, and Diego answered her sharply. I was beginning to regret that I hadn't paid more attention to learning real world Spanish. I just hadn't needed it in my hometown of Kansas City.

"What is it?" I demanded.

César pointed at his son. "Diego mahk dee deal wid bandeets. Day loose men. Day are wanting plane or keel us." His disgust was obvious, but his English was even more heavily accented than his son's, and I had no idea what he was saying.

"What?" I asked.

"Bandits want your plane," the girl said. "Diego made a deal with them, and they want it because the deal didn't work out. They will kill us if we don't give it to them."

"No way." I slid my pistol from its holster, glad my Renegade training meant I carried extra magazines and more target practice in a month than most mortals had in an entire lifetime. "They are *not* taking my plane."

Cost aside, the plane was our way of rushing back

a cure we desperately needed for the husband of Stella Davis, one of our Unbounded Renegades. Bronson was dying of a rare autoimmune disease, and our lab here in the Mexican jungle had reported a breakthrough with a cure. But two days ago, the lab had been razed to the ground, and my team was tracking our scientists that we believed had escaped with the research. I wasn't about to let my people down, especially after what had happened at our stronghold yesterday. It was more than just the life we'd lost. Far more.

"You no understand," Diego shouted, punching his fist in the air. "Your friends keel their men. They no leave. They will keel you."

I pointed my gun at him. "What deal did you make?"

No one answered for a long moment. Then the girl said, "They were supposed to rob your friends."

That almost made me laugh. Against my younger siblings, Erin and Jace, and the experienced Renegades with them, an entire army of mortal bandits wouldn't have stood a chance. Unbounded can't be killed, not in the normal way. Head and heart and reproductive organs had to be completely separated. No two sections could remain attached or they would fully regenerate. Unique abilities made Unbounded even more powerful, but of course, these people knew nothing of Unbounded.

"You sold us out?" I spat at Diego. I was going to kill him! We'd paid them a small fortune to land here and to park the plane while we finished our business. The weaponry alone that we carried would have been attractive to any militant group, but I'd expected some honor in dealing with César, who I understood had worked with our Renegades in the past. Apparently, his son was greedy.

The girl was still studying me. "All the men who attacked your friends in that big vehicle died, except two who were tied up."

Big surprise there. "Just give them back their money," I said to Diego.

He shook his head violently. "No. They want more. They want the plane."

"Geeve me key," César ordered, holding out his big hand, palm up.

I backed away. "There is no key. It's numbers, and I won't give them to you."

"Then you die!" Diego growled. "One man against all them. You no succeed."

"You have guns," I jerked my head at the two rifles standing against the wall. "We can take them together. Or drive them away."

"No! No!" César shouted. He glanced out the window where the bandits were still gathered in a clump near a blue truck. "Day keel you! We no help or day keel us too."

As if they could hear us, the bandits began piling into their truck.

Above all, I had to hold the plane. Not just for Stella's husband, but for our team. The Renegades were all that stood between humanity and enslavement by the Emporium Unbounded, who considered themselves gods to the expendable mortals. The Emporium had murdered my wife and tried to kill the rest of my family to further their agenda. They'd tried to abduct my children for their breeding experiments. Now they were here in Mexico and were most certainly behind the attack on our labs.

The plane was our way to safety. There was only one choice.

I lunged for the girl, grabbing her and pulling her against me, my gun pressed into her side. "You will help me fight. You made a deal with us, and you won't break it. Now pick up those guns, or I'll kill her."

I must have sounded convincing because both men, nodding energetically, started for their guns. Suddenly, it didn't seem wise to be in the same room with them. "I'll watch the back door. When they come, I'd better hear shooting."

With that, I dragged the girl into the kitchen. It was a small place with only one narrow window opposite a black potbellied stove that looked like something from a frontier movie. Shutting the door to the other room, I shoved her into a chair. "Don't move."

She watched me, seemingly more curious than afraid. "You a good shot?"

"I guess we'll see." I wished I were wearing my body armor.

I slipped a picture from the pocket of my white T-shirt. My young children stared up at me, Spencer's thin face covered in freckles and Kathy's blue eyes looking so much like her mother's. They were in hiding with the rest of our Renegades until we regrouped after the Emporium attack. Safe for now, but as long as the Emporium existed, they would always be in danger. I slipped the photograph back into place.

My watch said that only two minutes had passed when the shooting began. I stepped to the back door, almost expecting the girl to bolt, but she remained sitting. As I opened the door a crack, a man came around the edge of the house. I fired, and he crumpled.

I felt sick. All the practice in the world hadn't prepared me for actually taking a man's life. I was a pilot by profession, not a killer. Not Unbounded. Just a regular guy, who chose to work with the Renegades in order to protect my children, to make the world a safer place. That might sound noble, but I'd seen what the Emporium had to offer, and there was nothing noble about fighting them. I fought simply because it was the only way humanity would survive.

Except these men weren't semi-immortal Emporium agents. They were mortal.

A movement inside had me turning my gun back toward the girl, but she already had a pistol in her hand. For a several seconds, we stared at each other while the *boom* of rifles came from the next room and from outside. I couldn't shoot her. She was innocent.

She whirled from me abruptly, breaking the window with her gun and firing at someone outside. I blinked, almost surprised to still be alive. More men were coming around the house, and I fired again and again. So did the girl. The faces ducked out of sight.

"Is there a way onto the roof?" I asked.

She started to shake her head, but then nodded. "You can use the window and climb. You will have to do it from outside. I will cover you."

If we made it out alive I'd have to ask her where she learned to speak such great English. Her words were accented, attractively so, but completely understandable.

Should I trust her? She could just let them kill me.

"Why are you helping me?" I asked.

Her chin lifted and for a moment she was fiercely beautiful. "Because those men killed my husband."

It was good enough for me.

# CHAPTER 2

"TAKE THIS." WITH ONE HAND, SHE PUSHED A HIGH-BACKED chair at me. "To help you climb."

Letting off a few shots, I sprinted outside to the window and threw down the chair. I vaulted onto the windowsill and from there onto the low roof. Much easier than I'd thought, thanks to our grueling training sessions with Ritter, our combat Unbounded, who was like Rambo times thirty. He and my sister Erin made a perfect couple, though she didn't know it yet.

Shots followed my progress, telling me the girl had fulfilled her promise. I squat-walked across the roof, shoving in a new magazine. Two men were dead out front and, with the one I'd shot, that meant only three more left.

Close to the edge, I got down on my stomach and pulled myself along with my elbows. I picked off two men hiding behind their blue truck before they realized I was above them. The remaining man scrambled for cover, but a shot rang out and he fell before moving two feet.

The girl walked into view below me, still holding her pistol. I wondered if she was happy with her revenge, or if it made her feel as empty as I was feeling. I moved to the edge of the roof and lowered myself down, jumping the last few feet as Diego and César burst from the house. I tensed, but neither tried to shoot me. They were talking a mile a minute again in Spanish. After the words slowed, together they began carrying bodies and tossing them into the back of the battered truck.

I lifted my brow and looked at the girl.

"They want to move them and the truck away from here," she said, "and then they want to hide. They are afraid the rest will come."

I groaned. "There's more?"

A hint of a smile touched her lips. "Not too many. We are lucky they hijacked the van that was here before they sent their men after your friends. Some of the bandits drove it to their hideout. That was why only six came for the plane."

In a rush, the dread was back. "They hijacked the van?" This was bad news. Very bad news.

Two of our allies, Tenika Vasco and Irwin Stafford, also Renegade Unbounded, had met the plane to take into custody the eleven Emporium agents we'd captured yesterday during the attack in Oregon. Each of our captives was Unbounded and, though temporarily dead or heavily sedated, would heal sooner or later. They were being transported to our prison compound here in Mexico where they would be reformed or stand trial for their crimes against humanity.

Or at least that had been the plan before the van had been hijacked.

The girl frowned as her brother and father passed us carrying another dead bandit. "I'm sorry, but they are saying that the bandits were bragging about killing the driver."

I clenched my fists, my mind searching for options. I hadn't been at the plane when Tenika and Irwin had arrived in the gray van and loaded the Emporium agents, but I'd watched them through my binoculars while Diego was arranging his "vedy good coffee," and Jace had filled me in by sat phone on the details before they'd left. He'd been excited because Irwin had been famous in Australia for wrestling alligators before he'd faked his death to hide that he wasn't aging. He had been assigned to Mexico until his face was forgotten by the rest of the world.

Tenika, on the other hand, was here from New York City, delivering her own Emporium prisoners. She had agreed to help Irwin, who was shorthanded at the prison, transport our captives because she knew we were pressed to find our scientists. I'd met the Angolan woman several times and had a great respect for her.

The bandits wouldn't know how to permanently kill

Tenika and Irwin, but they could put them out long enough to allow the Emporium captives to regenerate, and the Emporium definitely *would* kill or capture my allies.

I had to do something.

If I were Unbounded and had an ability, I might be able to track them myself, but as it was I would have to depend on technology. All Renegades had embedded nanochips in their bodies, programmed to prevent their immune system from rejecting them. The chips emitted a constantly changing pattern, traceable only by someone using the same set of algorithms that would take even a technopath months to decode—and by then the algorithms would have changed yet again. If Tenika and Irwin weren't already too deep in the jungle, I should be able to track them. The captives had also been injected with tracking devices.

Still gripping my gun, I strode away from the building, heading across the wide expanse of dirt for the plane. Reaching into my pocket for my sat phone, I put in the password and made the call to Ava O'Hare, our cell leader. She was also my fourth great-grandmother, and three hundred years old, though physically she was thirty-seven, a year younger than I was.

She answered immediately, which told me she was waiting for news. "Hey, Chris."

"We've got a problem. I need you to track our captives and Tenika Vasco."

A brief pause. "On it. I'm contacting the New York

cell now to have them check for Tenika's codes. What's up?"

"Bandits tried to take the plane. They didn't succeed, but I learned they grabbed Tenika and the guy from the prison compound a few hours ago. The bandits were probably looking for weapons and money, but if they've dumped the bodies . . ." I didn't have to finish. Ava knew better than I did what the Emporium agents were capable of if they recovered before our people did.

"Okay," she said, "I can't locate any of the captives' signals." Which had to mean the tracking chips had been deactivated or that they were under cover of the jungle and the overhead satellites couldn't locate them. I was betting on the trees.

After a few seconds, Ava added, "They can't find Tenika's signal either." No hiding the worry in her voice. "Marco's on the line with the prison compound now about Irwin." Marco was one of our former black ops mortal employees, and we'd left him and two others like him to help Ava protect Stella Davis, her husband, and my children.

Several seconds of silence and then I asked, "How is Bronson?"

"Not good."

"And Stella?" Stella Davis had paid a huge price at yesterday's battle—loss of the baby she was carrying. With Bronson on his deathbed, it was a horrible turn of events. We all knew she had wanted their child more than she'd wanted anything in her two centuries of life.

If Bronson died, their chances of having another child would be over forever.

I owed Stella. I would always owe her. She'd made the choice to fight, to save my children. When this was all over, I'd go home to them because of her sacrifice. I was determined to bring her the cure Bronson needed the minute the others tracked down our missing scientists.

"Okay, we found Irwin's signal," Ava said. "Pinpointing now."

I'd reached the stairs to the plane and began climbing, opening the door with the combination and my hand on the reader.

"He's only a few miles northwest of your position," Ava said in my ear. "Way too far for Ritter and Erin and the others to get to him, even if I could call them back. You'll have to go after him and see what happened. Could be the bandits just took the van and weapons and dumped the rest. They could all be nearby."

I didn't blame Ava for wanting the best-case scenario. I hadn't been on many ops—okay, I really hadn't been involved at all except for flying. All the fighting was left to the experienced mortals or the semi-immortal Unbounded. When Erin and Jace had been little, I'd taken care of them. Now that they had Changed, the roles were reversed. That took a lot of getting used to on my part because deep down I was still their protective older brother.

"I'll get supplies," I said, sealing the plane door behind me and striding down the aisle to the storage compartments located in the small kitchen at the back left side of the plane.

"Grab sedatives and extra curequick." She hesitated before adding, "Better take one of Ritter's bags."

I already had one in my hands. Ritter's bags contained everything a soldier could need in a battle: an assault rifle, extra ammo, several handguns, radios and earbuds, a change of clothes, and even a few grenades. I was stuffing the curequick into it now, along with food rations that Unbounded wouldn't need. They could absorb nutrients from the world around them, which I had to admit made me envious at times. A soldier who didn't need to eat but whose energy was continuously renewed was infinitely better in combat. No need to find or carry water. No worrying about how long a campaign might take.

But there were no Unbounded here, only me, and I was going after our people.

"I'm sending the coordinates to your phone," Ava said. "Let me know the minute you have eyes on them. Go slowly when you get close. The bandits may still be there or could have left a guard."

"Will do."

Hanging up, I stuffed a second water bladder into the bulging shoulder bag and began shedding my clothes, exchanging my jeans and T-shirt for a bulletproof vest and jungle camouflage. It was muggy here and hot, even in mid-November, at least it would be until night fell, but anything to keep me safe and unnoticed was worth it. The concern in Ava's voice had me jumpy, but I was glad she hadn't pointed out the fact that I could be killed. I was already made aware of that every day working with my siblings.

# CHAPTER 3

As I resealed the plane, the blue truck revved and left the building, heading not toward the plane but down the dirt road that bordered part of the runway. César's sedan followed. So much for my plan of taking the blue truck at least part of the way. The nearly three miles to Irwin's location wouldn't take me long to cover on foot, but every second could mean greater problems for Tenika and Irwin. I started toward the road.

I couldn't help but think of my children. I joined the Renegades to make a difference, to find justice for my wife, Lorrie, and because only the Renegades understood what happened to rip our lives apart. I believed in this fight and would give all I could to it, but ultimately my children had to be my first priority. It was comforting to know I wasn't the only one who felt Kathy and Spencer were important. The children weren't really just mine anymore, but a part of our larger family of Renegades, something they desperately needed after losing their mother.

A high, whiny sound of a motorbike cut off that vein of thought, and I turned around, grabbing the assault rifle hanging over my shoulder. It was a small bike, the kind that most American men would laugh at and refuse to own. I eased my finger off the trigger when I realized that riding it was the girl from earlier.

She came to a stop next to me. "You will go after your friends?"

I nodded.

"I can take you."

"Just give me the bike. I'll bring it back or pay you for it."

She shook her head. "I want to come. They killed my husband."

"Don't you understand? They don't care about you! You can't make a difference against them."

"We made a difference back there," she retorted. "And you are only one. Together we are stronger."

"Give me the keys."

In answer, she turned off the bike and put the keys down the front of her shirt, giving me a compelling glimpse of cleavage.

I was tempted to throw her off the bike and take the keys, but I wasn't that kind of man, and I didn't have time to convince her. Besides, she *had* helped me back at the building.

"You can go partway," I said. "Then you let me go on alone to check on my friends. I can't have you putting them in danger. Deal?"

She wanted to protest, but apparently something in my eyes convinced her I wouldn't bend. Nodding, she scooted back on the bike, fished out the keys, and handed them to me.

I blinked in surprise, both at her trust and the fact that she would let me drive. Not something the women in my current life would even think about offering willingly. *Maybe I'm living in the wrong country,* I thought.

"No, you drive," I said. "I'll keep a lookout."

Her eyes widened in a way that made me feel strangely protective. She'd been married and was a widow, so maybe she wasn't as young as I'd first thought. A woman, not a girl. She was certainly beautiful, even if in a way that was completely opposite to my blond-haired, blue-eyed wife.

Lorrie. I wondered if the pain would always come whenever I thought of her.

Looping the assault rifle over my head, I pulled out a pistol instead. We were off, the air once again filled with the whiny complaint of the small engine. But it drove well on the dirt road and, if it didn't alert every bandit in Mexico with the sound, we would get there in minutes.

I became acutely aware of my left arm draped loosely about the woman's waist. I didn't even know her name. She had a pistol tucked into the back of her tight jeans. No holster.

"Okay, stop here," I yelled in her ear a few minutes

later. She eased to the side of the road and turned off the engine. The abrupt quiet sounded almost loud.

"Wait here," I said. "I'll come for you when it's safe. Or you can go back to the house and wait for me."

Her mouth pursed in a scowl and her dark eyes narrowed, but she nodded. "I'll wait here."

I hurried away, straight into the woods, when really I needed to go further along the road. I couldn't have her following me. After a minute, I altered my direction, ran hard for stretch, then began my real approach. Slowly now. Careful. Eyes searching.

I could hear nothing but the occasional cry of a bird; whatever had happened here had frightened away the animals. My chest felt tight. I checked the GPS. Irwin should be just up ahead a few yards off the road.

Even more cautiously, I crept forward. I didn't know what I'd do if the bandits were still there, but if they were, I wasn't about to leave Irwin with them, Ava's orders or no.

The trees were thinning now, and I scanned the area carefully. *There,* I thought. I could see an arm poking out from under a bush. I circled around, trying to locate any attackers, but no one else seemed to be anywhere near here. Just to be certain, I hunkered down and waited, my heartbeat slowing as I breathed deeply.

After five minutes, I was convinced the bandits had abandoned Irwin to the animals, which thankfully hadn't yet appeared. I rose and pushed my way through the brush, looking under the lush greenery to see if I could locate Tenika as well. But there were enough breaks in the trees overhead that if she'd been nearby, Ava would have been able to locate her using the satellite.

I pulled Irwin from under the bush. The blond man was drenched in fresh blood. He'd been shot in the chest and again in his leg, where shards of bone jutted from his blood-soaked jeans. He had no heartbeat, but already the wounds were beginning to heal, and the curequick in my bag would help him regenerate even faster. I injected the substance around each wound and then sat back on my heels. Nothing left but to report the bad news to Ava.

She answered before my first ring finished. "Hello?"

"I found Irwin, but no sign of Tenika yet."

"What's his condition?"

"Not too bad. He bled out from a chest wound. Heart stopped beating, but they missed hitting it directly at least."

"No head wound?"

"No. But his leg's pretty badly busted up. I can see bone."

"With the curequick he should regain consciousness soon. See if he can tell you anything. How much did you give him?"

"Two syringes. One near each wound."

"Wait five minutes and give him two more. Meanwhile, search the area for clues."

"Okay, but they've taken everything of value from him—guns, phone, the van. You'll need to let his people know."

"We figured as much. They're waiting to hear from us."

I broke the connection, wondering what she expected me to find. I'd been training with the Renegades for two months now, but we hadn't covered tracking in a foreign jungle. Or if they had, I'd been taking care of the kids that day.

I walked around, noting the torn leaves and signs of a struggle. Tire marks showed where they'd been forced off the dirt road. At some point Tenika and Irwin must have left the van. One thing was certain, they hadn't been defeated easily.

I followed the tire marks of the van through the jungle foliage, trying to determine where it met back up with the road, if it did at all. Some distance away from Irwin, another smaller road appeared, deep under a canopy of trees. Near this, I found four more bodies, heaped on each other like refuse.

"Hello," I said. These were our captives. Or some of them.

They still had no pulse, but they didn't look worse than when they'd left our plane. All the blood on them was long dried and their wounds on their way to full healing. The bandits must have thought them dead. But why had they kept the other seven? Maybe because they'd started breathing again. If they had only taken those who were alive, it could mean they kept Tenika as well.

All our Emporium captives had been heavily drugged, but in another day, or maybe by morning, their bodies would have cleared the drugs from their systems. I needed to find them before then.

But how?

A movement in the trees sent me scuttling backward, my gun drawn. Sweat dripped from my hairline down the back of my neck as I wondered if the bandits or one of the less-damaged Emporium agents had returned to consciousness.

# CHAPTER 4

**"D**ON'T SHOOT!" CAME A FEMALE VOICE. "IT'S ME, MARISA."
I had no idea who Marisa was, but the slamming
in my chest abated slightly as my heart decided I wasn't
in immediate danger. "Come out!"

The woman who'd brought me here emerged from the
brush onto the small road, her blue tank top contrasting
noticeably with the dark green jungle decor. Her pistol
was in her hands, though it was pointing at the ground—
for the moment.

Okay, so I did know her, and I wasn't really that
surprised to see her. I stepped out from my tree. "I
thought I told you to stay with the bike."

One delicate shoulder lifted in a shrug. "I did. It's just
over on the main road. I walked it here."

I couldn't really blame her for disobeying when I'd
planned to disregard my own orders and fight the bandits

if I had to in order to save Tenika and Irwin, but it unnerved me all the same. If anything happened to her, I'd feel responsible.

Marisa hesitated several long seconds before taking a few steps and squatting down to stare at the captives. "They're dead. Who are they? Why do they have that . . ." She struggled to find the word. "Metal bracelet."

"Shackles." I shook my head, knowing she'd never believe how dangerous they still were. "I'll come back for them later, but first . . ." I delved in my bag for more of the drug that had been especially prepared to sedate Unbounded. I couldn't kill them with it; in fact, an overdose would only buy me a few more hours. As I injected the drug, the woman stared at me as if I'd left my brain back at the plane, which maybe I had.

"Come on," I said roughly.

She followed me through the brush back to where I'd left Irwin. I knelt down and began giving him another dose of curequick. Afterward, I checked his neck for a pulse, my fingers looking white against his deeply tanned skin. A faint beat awarded my effort. It wouldn't be long now.

"He's dead," she said, disgust lacing her voice. "Can't you see that? What did you give him? It's different than what you gave the others. The needle is bigger."

"Since you're so good at observation, can you tell me what happened here? I'm looking for the woman that was with him."

"You mean the black one with all the long braids?"

"How did you know?" Because Marisa definitely hadn't been introduced.

"You're not the only one who has binoculars." With another uneasy glance at Irwin, she stood and began looking around, studying the signs of the struggle as I had. After a time, she sighed. "There's not much to see. They were pushed off the road, and they took cover behind the van. I see many empty shells."

"Shells. Right." I hadn't even noticed.

She cocked her head, her voice devoid of emotion. "I'm sure they have her. They always need women, so they'll want to keep her. She might have a chance to run away after they have their fun."

"They'd keep her alive?"

"For a while at least. If she doesn't fight too much." The emotionlessness tone was emphasized by a deadness in her beautiful eyes, and I wondered what else they'd done to her when they killed her husband.

I forced myself instead to think about Tenika. If she was with the bandits, it might be a good thing. Her talent was hypnosuggestion, which she used in her cover job as a psychologist. If the bandits listened to her, she might be able to convince them to let her go and to turn over the Emporium captives. The bandits wouldn't know to muzzle her unless one of the agents somehow regained consciousness.

"Tell me about the bandits," I said, settling in the vegetation a couple feet away from Irwin. "What's their gig?"

"Gig?"

"How do they survive?"

She sank down in the soft grass beside me, on the side away from Irwin. "Stealing, drugs, anything really. Some groups deal in slavery—mostly capturing the native Maya." She wrinkled her nose as if she'd caught a whiff of something nasty. "They take whole family groups, make them work for them."

"What kind of drugs?"

She shrugged. "All of it. I don't know."

The drugs made me feel uneasy, but I didn't know why it would trigger my alarms more than kidnapping. "Do you know where they live?"

Marisa frowned, staring at me with a worried crease between her eyebrows. "No." After a few seconds of hesitation, she added, "My husband found their place, the same bandits who did this. That's why they killed him."

"How long ago?"

"Two months." Her flared nostrils and clenched jaw told me that it still felt like yesterday.

Two months, the same amount of time Lorrie had been gone. "You should go home to your father and brother—or wherever they are."

"They can't protect me. They expect me to stay and cook for them, but I won't. I have an uncle who owns a ranch outside of Palenque. My mother's brother. I lived with him and his American wife when I was little after my mother died. I will go to him when this is over." Her gaze dropped.

I wanted to ask how old she was, but it wasn't something I felt I could do. "I'm sorry."

She shrugged. "Who is in the picture? The one you took out of your pocket earlier?"

I felt for it and passed it to her. "My children, Kathy and Spencer."

A smile chased the sadness from Marisa's face. "Oh, they are so nice. They don't look much like you, except the blond hair."

"Kathy takes after her mother. Believe it or not, when I was young, I had those same freckles that are torturing my son's face."

She laughed. "Then he'll be as handsome as you when he is a man." She lowered her eyelashes, peering at me from under them. She was flirting, but I didn't mind. It had been a long time since I'd noticed any woman flirting with me, though Lorrie had claimed many of the clients I'd ferried around had flirted like mad.

"And your wife? Do you have a picture of her?"

I did, but I had stopped carrying the photograph because it hurt too much. "She's dead," I said. "Two months ago. Killed by those men back there." I jerked my head in the direction of the Emporium captives. It wasn't those same men, of course, but others from the same group.

Her eyes opened fully now, and I could see they glistened with moisture. "That's why you killed them. I understand."

"Not me. I wish it had been."

She nodded. "That, too, I can under—"

A gasp from my other side cut off her words. I leapt to my feet and hurried to Irwin. He had a knife in his hand and sliced at me, his eyes rolling back and forth wildly

Marisa shrieked and jumped up, pulling her pistol with one hand and crossing herself with the other. Her mouth spilled long strings of Spanish. Cursing or prayers, I couldn't tell which.

"Stop!" I said, raising my hands in front of Irwin to show I was unarmed. "I'm a Renegade. Part of Ava's group. I'm here to help you."

He calmed immediately, despite Marisa's pistol and her continued flow of words. "All right," he said in a thick Australian accent. He shifted his body slightly, grimacing with the pain. "Fill me in."

"Marisa," I barked, "put that down!" I glared at her until some sanity returned to her eyes and her weapon lowered.

I turned back to Irwin and explained what had happened in a few short sentences. "I think they have Tenika," I finished.

"That's my bet. We'll have to go after them." He attempted to sit but gave up as his body convulsed in pain.

"You aren't going anywhere. Here. Let me help." I dragged him to a tree and propped his back against it. He panted through gritted teeth, his forehead furrowed with agony.

"You don't understand," Irwin said as the pain eased.

"Those bandits will wake up our prisoners with their drugs—they're quite proficient at knocking people out and waking them for interrogation. Once they discover the Emporium will pay to get those guys back, they'll make a deal."

"The Emporium won't pay bandits. They'll just kill them." If it weren't for Tenika and losing the captives, I'd just leave them to it.

"Probably. Unless they think they can use them in the future." Irwin grimaced down at his leg. Already the shards were less noticeable as the new bone regrew and knitted itself back together.

"I have some pain killer," I offered. His body would get rid of it quickly as it did anything else, but given enough, he ought to experience some temporary relief. "I gave you a small amount already in the curequick, but I have some separate. Injectable."

Irwin waved the suggestion away. "Look, we have to go after them. We're shorthanded at the prison. It'll take hours before I can get someone here, and by then we might lose their trail."

"Trail? There is no trail. They got on a road, and from there we have no idea where they went." I glanced back at Marisa for confirmation. She'd fallen silent, but her face was frozen, her pistol in a death grip—thankfully pointed at the ground. I wasn't sure she even heard me. "They have several hours on us already."

"I *can* track them." He said it with such confidence that I had to smile.

All Unbounded were arrogant to a point, even my own siblings. I believed it was mostly because the gene demanded it. Changing was just that: a complete Change. From mortal to semi-immortal, aging only two years for every hundred that passed. No more submissive tendencies, no more willingness to remain on the sidelines. Those who Changed had only the best genes. They were stronger, faster, and even more intelligent than the average human, and their individual abilities increased their confidence and usefulness.

But sometimes it also meant they didn't recognize their limits.

"You can't do that while sitting here in these weeds," I told Irwin. "And you aren't going anywhere until morning without transportation. So unless you've got more tricks up your sleeve, it looks like I'm going to have to start down that road without you and just pray I find Tenika before it's too late."

Irwin's mouth, still tight with pain, quirked up. "You'll go after her then."

"Do I have another choice?"

He shook his head. "No. But just so we're clear, I can track them. Even sitting in these weeds."

"How? You want me to carry you?" Judging by his pallor, he wouldn't even make it several yards on Marisa's motorcycle.

"Him." Irwin's eyes went past both me and Marisa, who also turned.

Amber eyes stared out at us from the midst of a large jungle bush, verdant with huge, deep green leaves. I had barely a glimpse of tawny fur and black spots before Marisa raised her gun and fired.

# CHAPTER 5

THE EYES VANISHED AS MARISA JUMPED BACKWARD INTO MY arms. Her slender body trembled.

"Take that gun from her!" Irwin ordered. "She scared him!"

Marisa whirled on Irwin. "Scared him! You're dead—or were. And that's a-a jaguar!"

"So?" Irwin frowned. "Woman, you might have just ruined our one chance."

Then I understood. Irwin's ability was to communicate with animals, or at least some of them, and I was willing to bet that creature knew more about this jungle than any of us.

I took Marisa's gun, removed the magazine, and handed it back to her. "No more shooting. Got it?"

She glared at me as she had when I'd left her with the bike, but she eventually nodded.

Irwin had shut his eyes, whether to try to communicate

with the animal or in pain, I couldn't tell. After a long minute, his eyes snapped open. "Go wait on the road. I'll call you when it's safe. Hurry, both of you!"

I grabbed Marisa's hand. "Come on!"

"You crazy?" she asked, her accent intensifying with her emotion. "He's hurt. That creature came because of the blood. He'll kill him again!" She stopped speaking, mouth slightly agape as the incongruity of her statement hit her.

"Irwin knows what he's doing. Half the world grew up on this guy wrestling alligators."

"What?" She crinkled her nose in a way that was becoming familiar and, if I wanted to admit it, rather attractive.

"Never mind."

She looked behind us, letting me drag her through the jungle foliage. We hadn't yet made it to the road when she tugged against me. "Look."

I stopped and saw that the jaguar was approaching Irwin, who held out a cupped hand. We waited, holding our breath as the creature reached him and pushed his face into the hand, nuzzling it. Soon Irwin was scratching the animal's neck.

Marisa was mumbling in Spanish and crossing herself again. I had to admit to a decided urge to begin mumbling to myself in some kind of foreign language because I didn't have words to describe this. It seemed only a few seconds passed until the jaguar pushed once more against Irwin's hand and bounded away into the forest.

"You can come back now," Irwin called, motioning to us.

We took no time in returning. "All right, mates," he said with a cheerful grin that almost hid his pain, "this is what's going to happen. My furry, four-legged friend—try saying that fast three times—knows where the bandits are, and he'll take you there. But he says to lose the motorbike. Won't be any use where you're going." Irwin frowned at Marisa. "And he doesn't want her to come along."

I had no intention of taking Marisa. "You're sure he knows the right group of bandits?"

"Yes. There's another group nearby, but their scent isn't here. You can trust him." Irwin gave a self-conscious smirk. "Well, as far as you can trust any wild animal."

So not at all. "Okay," I said.

"You can't be serious." Marisa stared at me aghast. "That thing will kill you."

"No, he won't," Irwin said. "I told him not to." To me, he added, thumbing in the direction where I had found the dead Emporium agents, "There's a smaller road over there. Just start on that, and he'll let you know when you need to veer off. He'll only show himself to get you to change direction or if you aren't going the right way. However, it's already near four, and it'll be dark by six. Could be sooner the deeper you go. I think you might make it before dark if you push hard, but you might not. It's hard to tell time and distance with animals."

"That's okay. I have everything I need." I hefted my bag. "I should take you back to the plane first."

He gave me another of his grins. "I'll be okay hanging out here for a few hours. If you're not back by morning, I'm coming after you."

He'd probably feel almost normal by then. "I already reported finding you," I said. "We're in contact with your people at the prison. That's how I found you."

"Good. I don't want them wasting time coming after me. Better they focus on getting a team together to back you up."

Or to do the job if I failed, he meant. "Take this." I gave him an extra pistol. "Just in case."

"The animals won't bother me," he said in that annoyingly confident tone. I decided I was beginning to hate his Aussie accent.

"It's for the two-legged kind." I turned and started through the forest. Marisa stumbled after me. From the corner of my eye, I got the merest glimpse of the jaguar up ahead, moving in the direction of the small road.

I waited until we reached it to talk to Marisa. "You heard what he said. You can't come. Besides, it'll be another few hours before he'll be well enough to travel. Then you can use the bike to take him back to your place. Take care of him until he can defend himself or until someone comes for him."

Marisa stared, backing away from me. "He is a ghost. I cannot. I—"

"Please," I said.

Without waiting for her reply, I turned and started jogging down the road. She didn't follow, which I took as a good sign.

I knew I had to make a choice about reporting to Ava what I was doing. If I didn't, it'd be grounds for expulsion from the Renegades, and I didn't want that. But I also couldn't have her ordering me back to the plane. Because if I had to wait for backup to search for Tenika, that might mean losing the captives altogether or at the very least a delay in bringing the cure to Bronson once our people tracked it down.

In the end, my conscience won out. I waited for a break in the trees overhead before slowing to a walk and dialing.

"Where are you?" Ava asked.

"I'm following a jaguar."

"What?" The amusement in her voice told me I'd caught her off guard. Good to know my young granny wasn't beyond surprise.

I gave her a quick rundown. "Irwin says his friends won't be able to get backup till morning and that the bandits have the ability of waking our Emporium friends."

"Chris, you know how dangerous this is."

I couldn't stifle my flare of anger. "What I know is that Stella didn't stop to consider her welfare when she protected my kids yesterday. I want all of this cleared up before Erin and the others get back with Bronson's medication."

She was silent for the space of a few heartbeats. "Okay, but reconnaissance only. Use good judgment. Follow our protocols. Report when you can."

The mark of a good leader was knowing when to back down, to let those under you take responsibility for their actions. I knew she didn't want me going, but she also knew I was going anyway.

"Will do," I said.

"Oh, and Chris."

"Yes?"

"Remember you have two very important reasons to come home."

Her words were quiet, but they might as well have been shouted from a loudspeaker. Or delivered with a drop kick to the gut. As if she had to remind me about Kathy and Spencer.

"I always remember that," I said quietly.

"Good." A faint click in my ear told me she'd hung up. I tucked away the phone and started jogging again.

I'd only gone five more minutes along the road when a low growl called my attention to the right. "I must be crazy," I mumbled, catching a glimpse of the jaguar's tawny coat with its black spots. My kids would be amazed when they heard this story—if I survived.

I had every intention of doing so.

I angled through the jungle, jumping over shorter bushes and circumventing the larger ones and the trees. I tried to maintain a good pace, keeping in mind that I really needed to find the bandits' encampment before dark. Hopefully, that also meant I'd arrive before they got around to waking up any of the Emporium captives.

When a stitch appeared in my side, I slowed down a notch, realizing that we were angling slightly upwards now. I heard what had to be a howler monkey, numerous bird calls, and the scream of another large cat. There were many creatures I never saw but only heard scurrying away—and not for my sake, but because of my guide. I was glad now for our rigorous training schedule because I would never have been able to keep up this pace two months ago.

The thought was like a knife turning in my stomach. Two months ago, Lorrie had been alive. Such a short time and yet it felt like years with all that I'd been through.

After thirty minutes of pushing through the foliage, I stumbled to a halt, my hand going to a tree for support. I had no idea how close an eye the jaguar kept on me, but he'd realize soon enough that I'd stopped moving. Mostly I needed to relocate my water to a more accessible position, allowing me to take more frequent sips without stopping. Having no way of knowing how much further I had to go, I'd better prepare for the worst. While checking my GPS, I downed a ration bar to keep up my strength. We'd gone mostly in a straight line since leaving the small road, though we'd recently taken a sharp turn around a raised bit of land.

My eyes wandered over the terrain. There was no evidence of human habitation. I might be standing on a spot that no human had ever stood on before. It was beautiful—no, gorgeous. Trees filled my vision, their green so bright and lush that it made something inside me ache. Why hadn't I brought Lorrie here before she died? Why had I been so preoccupied with making a living that I hadn't realized the best years of my life were already ticking away?

Stifling the urge to scream out my loss, I slapped at the back of my neck, squashing a mosquito that I hoped didn't carry some deadly virus. Maybe it was okay that I hadn't brought Lorrie here after all. She hated roughing it. A hotel in Paris would have been better. I should have sprung for that. Pastries, long walks along the Seine. A visit to the Eiffel Tower and to the Louvre to see the Mona Lisa.

I pulled back on my pack. *Hope you're watching for me,* I told the jaguar.

I'd taken only two steps when a faint voice called out my name. I stopped, listening. Nothing.

My imagination.

No, there it was again. Definite crying. Screaming. Female.

I hurried back the way I had come.

# CHAPTER 6

PULLING MY NINE MIL, I DROPPED MY PACK AS I RAN, MENTALLY cursing at the delay. I had a sinking feeling I knew who the woman was, but I didn't know who—or what—was making her scream. I didn't even know how she knew my name, though thinking about it now, I had introduced myself to her family back at their place.

Every day I worked with women who were tougher and stronger than I was, most of whom had centuries of experience. I was mortal, the older brother who was more fragile than his younger siblings. They always wanted to protect me. So it was an odd sensation to be hurtling through the trees with the hope of rescuing a woman. Of knowing I was the only one who *could* rescue her.

I didn't even want to think about being too late.

Seemingly long minutes later, I spotted Marisa through the trees, waving a big stick in her hand. Twenty feet in front of her, partially hidden by the trees, a jaguar looked ready to pounce. Without thinking, I sprinted through the remaining foliage, bursting out between her and the creature.

"Hey!" I shouted.

The animal yowled, sounding worse than a dozen tomcats fighting in an alley.

Marisa gasped. "He's going to kill me!"

I took aim with the gun. I had no way of knowing if this was the animal I had been following or a new one on the scene. Either way, I'd be sorry if I had to shoot it. The creature screeched again, its amber eyes digging twin holes through me. Should I fire the pistol into the air? If this was my guide, I might scare him off completely. Or he might decide I would behave better inside his stomach. A pistol shot might also alert the bandits of my approach, if they were near.

With a flick of his tail, the jaguar pounced—but into the forest instead of at me. For several long seconds, I contemplated my survival. Then I started after him. With a cry of dismay, Marisa scrambled after me.

I whirled on her. "I told you to stay behind. What, do I have to tie you up? Are you determined to get yourself killed?"

Or maybe she was working for the bandits. But no, she'd helped me kill them.

"Look," I said more calmly. "I have to keep going. Good people will die if I don't."

She glared at me. "You going to leave me here?"

"Go back to Irwin."

"What about that *diablo?*" She glanced in the direction the jaguar had disappeared, her chest heaving in real terror. Devil. That was one Spanish word I knew.

Guilt waved through me. I shouldn't have accepted a ride on the motorcycle in the first place. If I hadn't, she wouldn't be anywhere near here. Even if that jaguar was the one I was following, it might return for a soft meal. I'd have to give up another gun, unless she still had hers and I could return her magazine. "You can't keep up."

"Try me." She pushed past me, leaping over the brush with a grace that reminded me of the jaguar.

She was right, of course. I couldn't leave her in this remote place any more than I could leave Tenika to face the bandits alone. I sprinted to catch up, pulling ahead of Marisa and leading her back to where I'd dropped my pack. The crushed leaves of the plants made the trail easy to follow. No wonder she'd been able to track me. Her eyes followed my movements as I picked up my pack, the tip of a red tongue wetting her lips. She was breathing even harder now, and I had trouble looking away from her heaving chest.

I offered her the water tube, and she took it gratefully, opening the end with a practice that told me she was familiar with hydration packs. She took two steady pulls and gave it back.

"Better wear this," I told her, pulling out a camouflage T-shirt. As much as I hated to cover her up, she was like a neon sign in that blue tank—and it was better to keep my mind on the op instead of on her curves.

She pulled it on with a little roll of her eyes, telling me she'd noticed my interest. Not meeting her eyes, I tossed a ration bar at her before taking off again. I couldn't see or hear the jaguar, and I hoped he hadn't abandoned us all together. If he had, it was going to be a long night.

We'd gone another twenty minutes in the same direction before I glimpsed the jaguar again to the left. "That's right, buddy," I murmured, turning in that direction. "Good boy."

"Can we walk for a moment?" Marisa asked.

So far she'd kept up, and if I was really truthful—which I didn't plan on being—I'd gone faster with her watching my progress. I could do with a rest myself.

"Okay," I said, passing her my water tube. "Do you have any idea how far away they might be?" The bandits had taken the van and had a few hours on us, but since they had to use the little road instead of cutting through the jungle, maybe we wouldn't get there too far behind them.

Marisa thought for a moment. "Not too far. They have come and gone to my father's place in maybe thirty minutes, and the road isn't good. It winds back and forth like a snake."

"Okay, we'd better start being more careful then." Irwin had estimated that we'd make it before dark, and the light was beginning to fail. We'd also run a good way, which maybe Irwin hadn't counted on. The last thing we needed was to accidentally run into the middle of their camp or alert their lookouts.

Now that I was thinking about lookouts, I wondered how I could make sure we didn't get picked off before we realized we were near the hideout. Unfortunately, I didn't speak jaguar like Irwin.

I held back a large leaf so it wouldn't smack Marisa in the face. She smiled her thanks, which made me remember how she looked in that blue tank. I shook the thoughts away. I was missing Lorrie, that's all. Couldn't blame a man for looking.

We hadn't hiked another fifteen minutes before the jaguar screamed ahead, much further away than I'd heard him before. There was a shout and the bark of an automatic rifle.

It looked like we'd found the bandits.

Something came at us fast, the foliage rippling like a wave. I grabbed Marisa and pulled her into the shelter of a bush. The jaguar sprang into view, landing in front of us with a deadly snarl. For several seconds he stared at us, then snarled viciously again before bounding away, disappearing the way we'd come.

I waited, the woman in my arms trembling, but no one came after the jaguar. "What happened?" she whispered.

"I think we've found the camp, and it looks like the bandits aren't crazy about chasing Irwin's friend."

"Crazy like you, you mean."

"Hey, don't knock what works."

"Don't knock?" She arched a brow.

"Never mind." She couldn't know that I'd seen stranger things than an obedient jaguar since I'd joined the Renegades. My sister could sense emotions and thoughts, my brother could run almost faster than I could follow with my eyes and fight ten mortals without breaking a sweat. Stella could control three high-powered computers at once, processing more information than an army of nerds, and at the same time carry on an intelligent conversation with me.

"Who is she?" Marisa asked softly. "The woman who puts that expression on your face."

She was right, however much I didn't want to admit it. If anyone ever told me I'd be interested in another woman when my wife was only two months dead, I would have thought they were insane. Lorrie had been everything to me from the moment we met. Every day we'd been together, I'd known she was a ten on a scale where I hit maybe only a four or a five. Sometimes at night I'd watch her sleep until I couldn't stand not touching her, and then she'd awaken and we'd make love, and I knew that I would never stop loving her. I'd always prayed she wouldn't get up one morning and realize what a mistake she'd made in marrying me.

I wished Lorrie had been the one to survive that horrible day, my first encounter with the Emporium, but she hadn't, and Marisa was right that there was someone else: Stella, who was fighting for the life of her aging, mortal husband, Bronson. I'd be lying if I let myself believe that I was only here because of what she'd done for my children. I certainly wasn't risking my life for Bronson, though I liked the man well enough. No, I was here in this jungle because Stella's happiness meant more to me than almost anything, and she loved Bronson as much as I'd loved Lorrie.

"What's she like?" Marisa took my silence for agreement.

I closed my eyes, pushing back the images that threatened my control. Stella Davis was half Italian, half Japanese, with the drop-dead gorgeous looks men dreamed about—I know I had. She was also a talented technopath who could manipulate electronic information at a rate that wasn't conceivable to even most Unbounded, much less mortals. Yet it was her kindness, not her intellect or beauty, that had helped me keep things together during the dark days after Lorrie's murder, when at times I hadn't believed it possible to go on.

I couldn't pinpoint the moment my feelings for her had changed from gratitude to . . . something more, but not for a second did I fool myself that I had a chance with her. Not only because Bronson still lived but because I would die too soon, just like Bronson. Even with the cure for his disease. He was already in his seventies, and old age would eventually win out. No way would Stella be stupid enough to replace a mortal lover for another one who would leave her again.

"There is no woman," I said.

Marisa tilted her head, staring at me for a long moment. Then she asked, "What now?"

"We go slowly. I doubt the jaguar went into their camp, so that shot must have come from a lookout. Keep close." I eased forward, this time taking care not to leave a trail. I indicated for Marisa to do the same.

We heard the men before we saw them, and I eased behind a tree and glided along its leafy branches to the cover of another tree where two men came into view. They looked as brutal as the ones who'd tried to steal my plane. One was gesturing and the other laughing.

"Can you hear what they're saying?" I asked Marisa.

She shook her head. "I think maybe they talk about the jaguar."

"They may have more lookouts." We watched as the men finished their discussion, then one headed away, while the other shimmied up a tree.

"Only one lookout, I think," Marisa said. "He can see everything from up there."

We'd have to be sure he didn't see us before we took him out. I moved slowly around my tree until it was between me and the lookout bandit. "Looks like we've got a pretty good view of the camp," I whispered.

Marisa edged over to sit beside me. From where we sat, the ground angled downward slightly into a gentle valley, just large enough to accommodate one small, low-slung cabin, one large tent, several smaller tents, and an outdoor cooking area. There were also a couple motorcycles, a beat-up truck, a car, and the missing van, which looked decidedly worse than the last time I'd seen it.

The man who had been with the lookout disappeared into the big tent. I eased out my binoculars and had a closer look, but there was no one else in sight except two women who were cooking over a fire. They both appeared haggard and were wearing dirty clothing. The younger one was openly crying. Every now and then the older woman would stop working to offer comfort, her eyes glancing nervously toward the tent.

"She must have lost her man today," Marisa said, her voice dull and expressionless. "Or the one protecting her."

"What will happen to her?"

"Another will take his place. Women are in short supply." Again that dead tone that ripped at my heart. I remembered now when I'd heard it last: in my own voice after Lorrie had died and I'd been trying to figure out how to tell the kids.

Marisa had pushed so close that I could smell her sweat, but it didn't turn me off. In fact, I wanted to pull her closer and protect her. I wondered again how old she was, and if she would ever love another man or if she would mourn her husband until it was too late to matter.

Or was I thinking of Stella again?

A movement directed my attention away from Marisa to the tent below where a man was emerging. With him were two other bandits and one of the Emporium agents, hands still shackled, but awake. The agent was a large black man who had been shot in the hip, if I remembered correctly, then knocked unconscious by Ritter during the fighting yesterday. He had to be held upright by the men, his legs dragging behind him uselessly, also still shackled.

The Emporium agent was talking urgently as they pushed him to the ground several feet away from the women, and the first bandit pointed a gun at his face, barking something I couldn't hear. The agent fell silent. The other bandits grinned at his arrogant, angry face. If the captive was gifted in combat, it wouldn't be long before all the bandits were dead, shackles or no shackles. Their women would likely end up murdered as well.

The women began serving something in bowls to the bandits, who sat down to eat on a felled log that seemed intended for that purpose. The man with the gun waved away the proffered bowl and kept his weapon aimed at the Unbounded.

I lowered the binoculars. "I see only three men and two women, but there's no telling how many might be in the tents or cabin. And we're already losing the light. I'm thinking we should take out the guy in the tree and move in to see if we can learn more."

She shook her head. "They'll be sending someone to give him food. Let me see." I handed her the binoculars, and in the next second, she gave a swift intake of breath. The darkness was falling fast now, and I wasn't sure if I was imagining the paleness that seemed to creep into her dark skin.

"What's wrong?"

"Nothing." She pushed the binoculars back at me. "There will be at least one more in the tent with the woman and the others you seek, if they are here."

"We need to hit them before they realize what's coming. That guy down there is either their leader or he's taken over now that their leader is gone. He doesn't look stupid."

"No, he's far from that." Marisa's voice was strained, as though she could barely form the words.

Now I understood. "So he's the one."

She nodded, her jaw clenched so tightly it must hurt her face.

I put a hand on her shoulder. "You stay here. I'll get closer to the lookout. Don't worry. I'll wait to see if they feed him first. After I take care of him, I'm going down to look around. I have to see if Tenika and the others are here or if they've dumped them somewhere else."

If they had dumped them, what was I going to do? I couldn't risk my mission to take revenge for Marisa, however much I wanted to wipe that hurt from her face. I'd have to find the road they'd driven here on and back-track along it, hoping the wild animals hadn't beaten me to the bodies.

Still, some feeling told me they were in that tent. I had to know what was going on inside it sooner rather than later. Ritter had always taught us to follow our gut instincts, and that's what I planned on doing.

Before leaving, I typed out a message on my sat phone that would send automatically if I ever got into a clear spot where it could connect with the satellite. I knew Ava would have been tracking my implant, and I'd tried to walk in the open when possible, but the jungle was dense and I really didn't know if she'd be able to direct Irwin's friends to my location in the morning. Irwin might have to find another jaguar, and by then Tenika and the others could be anywhere.

*No, I'm going to free them tonight.*

I had to. Before it was too late.

# CHAPTER 7

MARISA WAS RIGHT ABOUT WAITING ON THE LOOKOUT. One of the men soon came in search of him, not with food, but to relieve him. I debated taking them both out right there, but I needed more time to find Tenika—time I might lose if the lookout didn't return to camp on schedule. I let him go, hoping I wouldn't regret it later.

This lookout hadn't gone up the tree like the previous one, but was pacing in front of the tree. His movements were taut and angry, and I couldn't help wonder who he'd lost today. But I didn't feel sorry for him for long because he'd chosen a life that exploited others and fed on their misery.

I took out a tranque gun because I was still feeling sick over the other men I had killed. I'd loaded it with double the dose. Not enough to kill a man his size, but enough to make even an Unbounded sleep for a few hours. The bandits might be out as long as twenty.

I aimed carefully, using the scope. A dot of red appeared on his back, showing me where it would hit. I pulled it a bit higher. He stiffened as the needle entered the base of his neck, but he didn't have time to turn before he crumpled into the vegetation without a sound.

Slipping through the foliage, I pulled him over my shoulder and carried him some distance away, tucking him under a bush. They wouldn't find him until morning—if there were any bandits left to search. I didn't think animals would be a problem this close to the camp, but you never knew.

The thought made me stop for a minute, staring back at the bush. *You can't worry about him,* I told myself. *Find Tenika.* Of course, it really wasn't for her. It was for Stella. I had to finish up here and be ready to take that cure home to Bronson.

I moved through the trees, gradually and without sudden movements that might catch the eye. The darkness had closed in and I was relatively sure those around the cooking area couldn't see me because of the light from the fire.

The leader was seated across from the Emporium agent now, and they were talking earnestly. They offered him food, which took him several seconds to accept. I could imagine his disgust at the campfire cuisine—Emporium agents were notorious for their fine dining. People who didn't need to eat could afford to be very picky. But this captive couldn't afford to alienate the bandit before he got free or succeeded in awakening more of his people. So far he was still securely tied, and that showed a cunning on the part of the bandit, which didn't bode well for my overall mission but that was working in my favor at the moment. No way did I want that Unbounded freed.

The young woman again attempted to hand a bowl of food to the leader, and this time he took it. From my new position, I saw that the woman was pregnant, her belly jutting tellingly from her thin figure. This didn't stop the former lookout, who'd arrived at the camp, from slapping her on the bottom and making a comment that had her scurrying back to the older woman.

*I should have killed him.*

I needed to be careful about such feelings, though, because emotion tripped up the mind and caused mistakes. Besides, I didn't know the woman's loyalty. Maybe she was here by choice.

I sidled around to the back of the big rectangular tent the men had come from earlier. It wasn't the usual nylon kind you could buy at Costco or Walmart or any local camping store but was made of thick leather sewn together with leather strips. The tent reminded me of a sturdy Indian tepee in the shape of a large army tent. While the bottom edges of the leather were held to the ground with wooden stakes, the poles themselves were rebar cemented into the earth—so not a transitory structure. Obviously the tent was built to endure both time and tropical storms, and the tiny valley and trees gave it added protection.

It was still a tent, and it didn't take me long to find a gap in the leather. Inside, the space was dark except for the light coming from a stone fireplace set along one of the walls, complete with a makeshift chimney. In the corner closest to me, I could see lumps on the ground that were obviously the Emporium captives, laid out unceremoniously on the packed earth. A guard stood over them, though none appeared to be moving, except for the slight up and down motion of their chests.

Closer to the fireplace, a figure sat on a solitary chair, but the person's identity was blocked by a second guard standing in front of the chair. It had to be Tenika sitting there, and she appeared to be conscious. Beyond her was an uneven row of cots, complete with mosquito netting.

Three bandits out front, two in here, plus the two women. Not a lot, but the conscious Emporium Unbounded changed everything. I could use Tenika's help taking the camp, if she wasn't too badly wounded. That meant I had to start here. Quickly, before their leader made his deal and Tenika was put out of the picture.

The guard in front of Tenika leaned over and said something into her face. I caught a glimpse of her narrow braids as she tried to respond through the gag tied over her mouth. Her hands were also tied and one shoulder sported a white bandage stained with a copious amount of blood. The guard said something to his companion and grunted, making an obscene movement with his hips. They both laughed.

I leveled the tranque gun and sent a dart into the

guard next to Tenika. He crumpled. Before I could shoot again, the other guard ran over to her, talking fast and low. She lunged forward, bringing the chair she was tied to with her, and rammed her forehead into the guard. He brought his gun up, but she twirled and savagely smashed the legs of her chair into him. They both collapsed.

I was reaching for a knife to cut my way in when an exclamation behind me halted the motion. A fist slammed into the side of my face. As I fell against the tent, I caught sight of the first lookout, the one I should have taken out when I'd had the chance. His pants were partially unbuckled.

Just my luck I'd chosen the side of the tent near their latrine, though it was logical since the area behind the tent was the farthest from the middle of camp and the most private—exactly why I'd chosen it.

He knocked the tranque gun from my hand before I could pull the trigger, but I did the same to him before he had his pistol halfway out of his holster. In a flurry of fists, we clashed. He hit my shoulder, I got his chin. Blood spurted out his nose; my lip split. He attempted to use a dried branch to club me; I used the same branch to smash his knee. He was about my size and the meanness in his eyes testified of more kills than I could imagine, but I had been trained by the best.

He tried to step back and call out for help, but I punched him hard enough to steal his breath. I followed with a kick to his already damaged knee, then an elbow to the head. He managed to plant a fist in my stomach in a move that might have been fatal if he'd been holding a knife. But he wasn't and the punch opened him for a potentially devastating blow. I pulled back my fist.

"*Para!*" Metal jabbed into the back of my neck.

I turned to catch a glimpse of the older woman who had been at the fire. Her eyes were determined, her teeth gritted tight. Her scrawny chest heaved, her worn gray tank top barely covering her sagging breasts. "Okay!" I slowly began to raise my hands, waiting for the right moment. The moment when she relaxed slightly, sure that the worst was over.

I hoped it would happen fast because the guy I'd hammered was grinning now, his bloodied face looking gruesome. In a moment, his fists were going to seek retribution.

Maybe bandit women didn't relax their guard.

Wait, there it was. The barrel pulled slightly away, and the woman began speaking in that same rapid-fire Spanish that everyone seemed to use without taking a breath.

I stepped abruptly back and to the side, my hand darting out to wrench the gun from her. She tumbled forward with the motion—right into the fist of the lookout as he lashed out at me. She collapsed instantly. Not looking twice at the woman, the bandit dived for a gun in the foliage. Since I already had her gun in my hand, I shouldn't have cared, but pulling that trigger would be stupid if I wanted to keep my presence a secret from his companions. I jumped on top of him, knocking him flat.

I felt for the gun he'd been after—my tranque gun. My fingers closed on the trigger just as I heard a shout from behind.

Suddenly my head exploded in pain and the world went black.

# CHAPTER 8

WHEN I AWOKE I LAY IN THE TENT NEAR TENIKA'S CHAIR. My eyes took several moments to focus and when they did, I almost wished I'd remained unconscious. This close to Tenika, I could see clearly what I hadn't been able to see before. Her dark face was a mess, as though someone had used it for a punching bag. The rag around her mouth was tied so tightly that her jaw was forced open. Not only had she apparently been shot in the shoulder, but her other arm had an open knife wound extending at least ten inches. Already congealing now.

Something wasn't right about that wound. These men used guns, and in hand-to-hand combat her skill would have far exceeded theirs. I suspected the cut had been inflicted after her capture, perhaps for torture. But torturing a gagged woman wouldn't be very productive, and if the gag was off she would have talked them into releasing her. Somehow the cut and the gag were related, but my mind was too foggy to connect the dots.

Tenika didn't meet my gaze but stared at someone behind me. I twisted to see who, and my body protested the movement in a hundred places that hadn't been hurt before I'd lost consciousness. Probably the lookout exacting his revenge while I was unconscious. I was lucky they hadn't let him kill me.

I really should have tranqued him in the woods.

As I rolled into the new position, I kept my hands first to my sides and then behind my back so they wouldn't see them and remember that they hadn't tied me up when I was unconscious. The guard I'd tranqued in the tent was still out and should be until morning without interference, and the man Tenika had butted with her head was also sprawled on the ground, his eyes shut. The bandit leader—who looked bigger up close—was standing with the lookout bandit I'd fought and the black Emporium captive who was awake. The captive was still tied and a gun was pointed in his direction, but he clearly found amusement in my predicament.

"I told you they'd send people after me," he said. "The only way to stop them is to let me contact my people and get out of here. We'll take the woman so you won't have to deal with her lying tongue. You saw how dangerous it was earlier." His words were jittery, and I wondered how many drugs they had shot him with to counter our sedative. "And look, that cut you made? You can see it's healing just like I said it would. Her face too."

"Shut up!" the leader growled in heavily accented English. "He cood be your friend and not hers."

"I am here for him." I gave the scowling black captive a smile. "Hey, dude, sorry the rescue didn't go as planned."

"Renegade scum," he muttered. He took a step forward, but the bandit leader stopped him with a jab of his gun.

So the captive must recognize me from the Emporium files, or maybe from when they'd held me prisoner after murdering my wife. Anger flooded me, though I knew this Emporium Unbounded wasn't directly responsible for Lorrie's death. He was only a drone in the Emporium army.

I shook my head, which instead of clearing my thoughts only made it pound that much harder. "Look," I said to the bandit leader. "If you deal with him, you will all be killed. That's a guarantee. He's not human like we are, and they don't care about humans. My people were taking him to a prison for his crimes."

"You shut up too!" The bandit growled. He paced a few steps, then paused and blurted out a stream of Spanish at his companion.

I shifted again, and pain blurred my vision for a few seconds, causing me to curl in on myself. Had the bastard broken my rib? But it was that position that allowed me to see Tenika's hands moving, her wrists tied to the armrests but her fingers free. Was that sign language? I wracked my brain. Wait. The movements resembled the signals Ritter drilled into us for ops, which I didn't usually pay much attention to, knowing that because of the kids and their need for me as a pilot, he would never let me put those skills to use in real life. But it was hard not to have some of it sink in. Tenika wanted me to free her. *Only two of them. Two of us,* she signed.

I had to give it to the Unbounded. They refused to give up easily, but then two bandits with guns probably didn't seem like much of a challenge to someone who couldn't be killed by a bullet. My mortality aside, she was right. We should be able to do something and, even damaged as we were, together we would be a match for them.

As the two men rattled off more high-velocity Spanish, the Emporium captive trying to insert a word or two during any pause, I very slowly pulled myself to a seated position, keeping my hands hidden. In the dim firelight, I could see that the ropes holding Tenika were tight but wouldn't be impossible to untie. One of my knives would have made shorter work of the rope, if they hadn't taken them from me.

I took inventory, patting down the special pockets of my camouflage. Everything was gone, except my bullet-proof vest and the magazine from Marisa's gun that was in the inner pocket of my pants next to the one that had been holding a grenade. I didn't know if they'd over-looked it because it was so small or because a magazine alone held no danger to them. I wasn't even carrying a gun that size. A small pile of weapons near the bandit leader's feet told me where my stuff had gone. My pack wasn't there, though, so my phone and extra weapons were somewhere else. Maybe outside near the back of the tent where I'd been looking through the gaps. Safe for the time being, but no use to me now.

What I needed was a distraction.

At that moment, the flood of Spanish ended and the bandit lookout headed for the tent opening. I wasn't sure where he was going, but Tenika's fingers spelled out reinforcements, so apparently she'd understood their conversation and knew the man was going for the other two bandits who were still outside somewhere.

I eased up on my knees and the bandit leader shifted his gun in my direction. He barked something more at the lookout, who paused and stared at me, an evil glint in his eyes.

*Great.* I had the feeling my life was about to get a whole lot worse.

A woman's scream sliced through my thoughts, freezing everyone into place. The lookout turned again toward the tent opening as Marisa burst through, followed by one of the remaining bandits. His gun jabbed into her back, his other hand gripping her arm. With her slender figure, she resembled a small child in Ritter's extra large shirt—a furious child, whose dark eyes sent a thousand needles in every direction.

"Javier!" she began, addressing the bandit leader. More words followed.

The bandit behind her snorted and pulled a second gun from his pocket, which I recognized as belonging to her. Javier took the weapon, checked the chamber, and began laughing. He asked Marisa a question and she pointed at me before responding. Javier laughed again.

I wished I knew what was going on, but I had more important things to worry about. Namely whether I should free Tenika's mouth so she could use her ability, or one of her hands with the hope that she could free her other hand and help me fight. *Hand,* I decided. If her hands weren't too ruined from fighting earlier, she'd be able to free her own mouth.

And where was the other bandit? Why hadn't he come inside to check out the commotion?

Still on my knees, I pushed closer to Tenika, letting my body partially shield my hand that was inching toward hers. Everyone still stared at Marisa.

Whatever Marisa had said made Javier order his subordinate to let her go, and he even tossed the empty pistol back to her. Then Javier motioned to Marisa, and she threw herself into his embrace. Her arms went around his neck as they began kissing. Not just kissing, but *kissing*. She practically sank into him, let him devour her.

My stomach dropped. Not at all what I had expected. No wonder she'd been so intent on getting to the bandit camp. I'd been a fool to believe her story.

Tenika's first hand was free, and I moved forward and over a bit to hide the fact that she was already working on her other one. But I wasn't the only person who had noticed. "The woman, she's—" the Emporium captive began, but before he could utter another word, Marisa turned from Javier's grasp and cracked her pistol into his jaw.

"Pig!" she shouted. "Your friends attacked the airport. They killed Javier's men! They almost killed my father and brother!" She turned and spoke to Javier in Spanish. I recognized only the word airplane and father.

"Ees thees true?" Javier barked at the Emporium agent. "Deed you do thees?"

As the Unbounded calculated the best response, Marisa's face turned to me, her dark eyes catching mine. Something shifted inside me. We both knew she'd lied, but what I didn't know was why. It wouldn't be long before Javier tracked down César and Diego to find out what had really happened. What would he do if he learned she'd lied? Maybe she was hoping he'd believe her and that César and Diego would back up the story. Whatever game she was playing at, she obviously had a history with Javier, one that involved ample lip-locking and a whole lot more.

From the corner of my eye, I saw Tenika shift, a signal that she was free, though the gag was still in place. Behind my back, I moved my hands in my own signal to her. I'd grab the lookout and finish the job I should have done right the first time. She'd be able to take out one of the others, but the fact that they had guns might mean the third would get us both before we finished. Worse, the man she'd knocked unconscious earlier was sitting up, still dazed, but awake enough to go for his gun when the fight erupted.

We had no choice.

I thought fleetingly of my children. I knew they'd be taken care of if I didn't return, but I was going to do everything I could to be the one to tuck them in at night and read them bedtime stories. I had to survive this.

Somehow.

Marisa was staring at me, and I jerked my head toward the tent opening. With Javier distracted, she could probably make it. She shook her head.

So she wasn't going to leave, but she hadn't alerted Javier to me either.

Then what the hell were those kisses for?

No time to consider. I gave a last signal to Tenika: *on the count of three. Two. One.*

I twisted as I jumped to my feet, jabbing my fist up under the ribs of the lookout bandit. His eyes widened, and his gun came around, but I twisted it out of his hand and punched it at his face. The blow landed with a solid clunk and he was down.

I turned to see that Tenika had made short work of the dazed bandit and was grappling now with the one who'd brought in Marisa. Even as I watched, she pulled his arm up so high behind his back that something snapped.

But it was Javier who caught my attention. He fired at Tenika. The first shot slammed into his own man, who dropped to the floor. The next shot hit Tenika in the stomach.

I fired at Javier, but as I did, a body rammed into me,

causing the shot to miss. Obviously, the Emporium agent had decided that Javier was preferable to me.

Even as I hit the still-tied man, Javier fired again, the bullet entering the captive's back. He crumpled and the gun swung around in my direction. "Don't move!" Javier screamed.

I had no choice unless I wanted to die. Tenika lay unmoving, out of the picture for now. Once the Emporium captives awoke, she'd be facing dismemberment or life imprisonment by the Emporium. I had to do anything I could to stay alive and get us out of this.

"Okay," I said, raising my hands. "Look, I'll pay you anything you ask."

"Too much trouble," Javier said. I was close enough to see the muscles in his arm move as he tightened his finger on the trigger.

"No!" Marisa shouted. She jumped toward him.

Without even looking at her, Javier's arm flung out and knocked her to the ground. She lay there in frozen terror, her eyes wide, her mouth open in a silent scream. "You like heem? No?" Javier waved the gun at me. He was staring at her, but I had no doubt the English was for my benefit. "I weel keel heem. You—" He said something in Spanish that was probably the same derogatory words that abusers around the world used to keep those they dominate in line. I wanted to kill the idiot in a slow manner that would give him time to relive every single thing he'd put Marisa through. That terror on her face wasn't just for me.

Slowly, I lowered a hand, feeling in my inner pocket for her magazine. My fingers closed around it.

Javier pulled a knife from his belt, saying something else to Marisa. A whimper escaped her throat. Darting a glance at me to make sure I hadn't moved, he brought the knife to her cheek.

"No!" I shouted.

His attention shifted to me. Crap. Real smart.

I bolted. A bullet whizzed past my ear. I reached the cots along the edge of the tent, dropping and rolling under one of them. Javier thundered after me. In seconds I would be a gonner. I bounced to my feet, picking up the cot and throwing it at him. As a second bullet ricocheted off the metal leg, I turned to Marisa, tossing her the magazine. "Run!" Whatever she felt for Javier, it was my fault she was here. My fault if she got hurt.

She caught the magazine, as if my act had finally freed her from her icy terror.

I hoped the bullets would give her a way to get past that last bandit, if he was still out there, so she could escape into the jungle.

I didn't have time to see if she'd obey. I dove behind the next cot, this time feeling fire explode in my stomach with Javier's next shot. *The vest,* I thought. The thing had been horribly uncomfortable during the hike, and it had better damn well done its job. I couldn't tell past the pain, but if it hadn't, there was nothing left.

At least I was still moving. With all my strength, I pushed against the black eating at the edges of my consciousness and shoved another cot at the crazy man who now stalked me. Then a third and a fourth. But suddenly there were no more cots. Just me and the man with the gun.

He grinned and bent over and put the gun in my face. "Now you die."

# CHAPTER 9

THREE RAPID SHOTS CAME FROM BEHIND JAVIER. BOOM, BOOM, *boom!* He toppled on me, his eyes staring in horror. I pushed him off to see Marisa standing over us, her gun in her hand.

"Marisa," Javier said, disbelief in his tone. "Marisa, mi amor."

"That is for three years of hell," she spat. "And this"— she emptied three more rounds into his chest—"is for my husband." Javier was long past hearing by the time a dry click signaled no more bullets, and I knew her words were for me. There was apparently a lot more to her story—and to those kisses.

I breathed a sigh of relief and came painfully to my feet. "Thank you."

"You are wounded." She hurried forward and took my arm. The sleeve was bloody, but the arm only grazed. My stomach and ribs hurt a thousand times more, but that vest had been worth every bit of discomfort it had caused me in the jungle.

"I'm okay. Let's see to my friend."

I hurried to Tenika, who was still conscious despite the steady flow of blood coming through her clothes. I removed my own shirt and bundled it against the stomach wound. She pushed her gagged mouth in my direction, saying something I couldn't understand, but the knot on the gag was impossible to remove, so I retrieved Javier's knife and cut through the cloth.

"Thank you," she said, the barest hint of her native Portuguese coloring the words.

"You okay?"

"I will be."

"I'll get you some curequick. Just let me check all these guys first before anyone else decides to use you for target practice." Or me.

"Good idea."

I covered her with a blanket before going around the tent to examine each bandit. Marisa began cutting one of the blankets with a knife so I could tie them all up. No way was I leaving any free. Except Javier, who wasn't going anywhere ever again. Occasionally, I caught Marisa's gaze drifting in his direction. Every time, her relief was clear, and I wondered again what had been between them.

"I took care of the man who relieved the first lookout," I said, "but don't forget we still have one more out there.

Did you see him when they captured you?" It bothered me that he hadn't yet appeared. If he was hidden in the trees with a rifle, getting out of here alive would be difficult.

"I saw him. He won't be a problem." Marisa's face held no expression as she spoke, but her eyes seemed haunted. I didn't ask her what happened. I hadn't heard any shots, but she likely had a few more tricks in her bag. I know I did. Renegades valued diversity.

I found my weapons and put my nine mil, the backup pistol, the grenade, and two knives back in their places, along with the extra tranque darts. "I'll be back in just a few minutes with your meds," I said to Tenika. With the last bandit out of the picture, I'd take the long way around the tent instead of wasting time cutting through.

"Uh, Chris," Marisa said.

I looked over to see that the other bandit woman, the younger one, had appeared in the tent doorway. She held a gun pointed in my direction.

My stomach tensed. I'd made another grave mistake in forgetting her, in discounting her because of her youth and pregnancy. She spoke now, her eyes wild. Her Spanish was slower than everyone else's, but I still didn't understand it.

"She says to drop your gun," Marisa told me.

The woman looked frightened but determined. The bulge of her child stood out sharply against the thin-ness of her small frame. I remembered Lorrie like that, a mixture of softness and angles, and so vulnerable. I didn't want to hurt this woman, but as long as she held that gun, we were all in danger. I wondered if Marisa could explain to her that we just wanted to leave and take the Emporium captives with us. But that wasn't really true. I wanted to be sure the bandits wouldn't bother anyone again. Short of killing them, my only choice was to turn them over to authorities.

The woman waved the gun, her volume growing now. I stepped closer, and her gun hand shook.

I was contemplating more diving and rolling, and somehow sweeping her feet out from under her—all without damaging her baby—when Tenika, still lying on the floor under her blankets, spoke in Spanish. Her voice held command, and almost instantly, the woman's expression relaxed. She lowered her gun and offered it to me. Closing the space between us, I snatched the weapon. Her face showed confusion now, as though she didn't understand how I'd gotten the gun.

Tenika kept talking. The woman's confusion vanished, tears filling her eyes as she nodded vigorously. A sob erupted. She curled in on herself, shaking, and I sprang forward to support her, afraid she would collapse. She sobbed as she clung to me, smelling of smoke, jungle, and roasted meat.

"Uh, what's going on here?" I asked. I hardly knew where to put my hands; I wasn't accustomed to holding women who weren't Lorrie, pregnant or not.

"I told her we'd take her someplace safe," Tenika

answered. "I just reminded her that she hated living here and that they'd kidnapped her in the first place. She wants to see her family."

I'd heard about Tenika's hypnosuggestion, but I had never seen it in play. She was impressive. I wondered how many bandits she'd won over earlier before someone got smart and gagged her. "Great. Now what?"

A smiled played on Tenika's ruined face. "Help her sit down on one of the cots. Then go get the curequick."

"Right." I didn't sense any compelling in her words, and I could say no if I wanted to—which I didn't—so I guessed she wasn't using her gift with me. I led the pregnant woman to one of the overturned cots. I made sure she was steady on her feet before turning it over, freeing it with a knife when it got stuck in the mosquito netting hanging overhead. I helped her sit, and then, with great relief, headed outside.

Marisa snorted her amusement as she followed me into the darkness. "Good thing no one will need that netting again."

"What, you planning on starting your own bandit club?" I asked.

"No, I . . ." the words trailed away. "Look, about Javier."

"You don't owe me anything." But a part of me felt she did.

"My husband had a farm on the edge of the jungle," she said, her voice losing emotion once again. "It was a beautiful place. Javier came to our farm when I was married only six months. He burned it all because my husband wouldn't pay his peace tax. Javier took me, though, because he knew my father and brother. He used me to get them to do things for him. And also because he wanted a woman. For the first year he kept me here in this camp like a prisoner. I hoped my husband would find me, but then I heard them talking one night." She stopped and the relative quiet in the jungle emphasized the stark pain in her voice.

"You learned he was dead."

"Yes. He'd tracked me here and Javier killed him—after making sure my husband knew I was now his woman. Javier kept me here for two years. Then I arranged a few incidents with his men—he's very jealous—and that convinced him I'd be better kept with my father and young brother. He'd come to visit." The revulsion in her face told me what she thought of those visits. "I had planned to steal their car and some extra gas to get me to my uncle's ranch. He has men and guns, but I was worried Javier would come for me there and cause him trouble."

"And then I came along."

"Then you came along," she agreed. "I should have told you."

*Ya think?* I wanted to say, but really, why should she have trusted me? Her father and brother had let her down, her husband hadn't been able to save her, and she'd been used for years by Javier. "You saved my life," I said instead.

"You saved mine. He would have killed me. If not today then another day."

On that we could agree.

We'd come around to the back of the tent, where the older woman still sprawled in the foliage. She had a heartbeat, but it was faint. "She's going to need a doctor." Still, I tied her wrists with a length of rope from my pack. I'd learned something with both Marisa and the pregnant woman: never assume anything. This woman had already held a gun to my head once. Between her, Javier, and the pregnant woman, I had almost grown accustomed to it. I definitely understood the adrenaline rush, which was maybe why my Unbounded siblings sometimes seemed to enjoy their battles with the Emporium far more than they should.

While Marisa hefted my pack, I carried the woman into the tent. After setting her on another righted cot, I gave Tenika tiny injections of curequick all along the cut on her arm, followed by two bigger injections in her stomach and shoulder.

"What about your face?" I asked.

"That bad, huh?"

Tenika was ordinarily a striking Angolan woman, but I couldn't see much of her African features behind the mass of bleeding flesh. Only her eyes and the tiny braids of her hair were halfway normal. "Kind of."

Her battered lips stretched in a smile that looked painful. "Better wait an hour. I'll be on a high in a minute as it is with this stuff." Tenika was speaking low, so that

Marisa couldn't hear, but Marisa was watching us curiously from across the room. "She doesn't know about Unbounded, does she?"

"She has to suspect. She saw Irwin come back."

"Ah. Well, you can start putting our Emporium friends in the van." The way she drawled *friends* almost made me laugh. "By the time you're finished, the bleeding in my stomach should have stopped enough for you to help me to the van as well. But make sure you get our weapons back. They took them into the cabin."

I went to work dragging our captives back to the van but left behind all the bandits. I'd stop at the first clearing we found and connect with a satellite to request that Ava send whatever passed for the local sheriff to pick up the bandits. Or I'd leave them for Irwin's guys. I'd accomplished what I'd set out to do.

Marisa shook her head in disgust at the apparently dead Unbounded captives, refusing to touch them, but she helped me with the weapons in the cabin, which were far more numerous than just those they'd taken from us. There was an actual bed in the cabin and a desk, and it didn't take much thinking to know this was where Javier had kept Marisa. I didn't object when she pulled a rifle over her shoulder and pushed a large box of bullets into a shoulder sack she carried. I also didn't say anything when she went to a loose brick in the cabin's fireplace and pulled out a metal box filled with cash. She deserved it, and it wasn't as if Javier could object.

Tenika was looking a lot better when we returned to

the tent to check on her. Even her face had knitted some, though the bruising was considerably darker. I injected a bit of curequick in several spots, and to her credit, Tenika didn't even flinch. I wondered how many times she'd been almost killed, or killed and come back to life. I didn't think it was something I'd ever get used to seeing.

I left Marisa talking to the pregnant woman as I helped Tenika to the van. Like most Unbounded, she didn't carry any extra pounds, but she wasn't a small woman by any means. It said a lot about her condition that she leaned on me at all. Despite the agony I glimpsed on her face, she didn't let out so much as a single groan.

When I'd shut the van door, Marisa and the woman were leaving the tent. "She's going with me," Marisa announced.

I blinked. "You're not coming back with us?"

"To the airport? Or to wherever you are taking those *things?*" She crinkled her nose. "I don't think so. They have a double gas tank in that sedan, and there's a gas can in the trunk. It's enough to get me to my uncle's ranch." The pregnant woman was already checking the gas can in the back of the car.

"Right," I said. "You sure it's safe?"

"The road should be safe enough with this." Marisa patted the rifle. "And now that Javier is gone, my uncle will welcome me on his ranch. It's a good place."

"Okay then." I wouldn't stop her from doing what she felt was best for her life.

She stepped closer until her hip brushed my thigh.

"Chris, I want . . ." Slowly, her face moved toward me, her lips seeking mine.

My heartbeat pounded loudly in my ears, and other parts of my body reacted without my giving them permission. I kissed her back, my arms closing around her slim frame. She was warm and soft and generous. I let it go on far too long before I finally reminded myself that I still had a job to do.

She smiled as I pulled away, her fingers brushing my lips. "You could come with me. You are a good man—I know that. I promise to make you happy, and I will love your children. They will be safe. I bet my uncle has use for a pilot."

For a moment I was tempted. Tempted to run away from the fight with the Emporium and the painful memories of Lorrie. Tempted to lose myself in Marisa's arms and in her world. Her recent life hadn't been pretty, but compared to what the Renegades faced on a daily basis, these bandits barely registered on their danger scale. I longed to raise my children in a place where they weren't at risk of losing someone they loved in a brutal manner that evoked nightmares even for adults. Where there was no chance of them being used in genetic experiments or exploited as pawns in a war that had already spanned centuries. I loved the idea of keeping this simple and generous woman by my side, of falling in love with her. The attraction was there—I'd felt it from the moment she'd appeared on the motorcycle. Maybe before that.

We could be happy. I could finish my duty, take the

cure back to Oregon, and return with my children to see where this relationship might take us. Marisa would never be Lorrie, but I didn't want to replace my wife. I wanted the pain to go away. I wanted safety.

Except there were also my feelings about Stella, however hopeless, and none of that was fair to Marisa. She deserved better. She deserved a man who couldn't sleep for thinking about her, a man whose heart was hers alone. She most definitely didn't deserve someone who was with her because he wanted to hide.

I kissed her again deeply, enjoying a last taste of her sweetness. "In another life, I would."

She gave me a wistful smile. "I know. I hope you will be happy."

I watched her drive away, wishing I had said yes.

# CHAPTER 10

I DIDN'T HAVE TO ACCOMPANY IRWIN AND TENIKA TO THE prison compound. By the time we'd retrieved the other unconscious Unbounded captives near the small road, Irwin was up and hobbling around the clearing where I'd left him. Tenika still looked a shadow of her normal self, but her face was already less hamburger and more bruise—a significant improvement from hours before back at the cabin. Irwin and I secured the prisoners, and by then several of his buddies from the prison had appeared, heavily armed.

"You're going to see to the bandits, right?" I asked.

"Sure thing," Irwin said. "We've already called in a few favors." He leaned closer and spoke so no one else could hear. "I'm glad my four-footed friend didn't attack you. I haven't had much experience with jaguars. It's crocs I know best."

"I'm really glad I didn't know that before I went after him."

"I thought you might say that." He chuckled and slapped me hard on the back, making me flinch. "Hey," Irwin said, "Drew over there is a healer. You want him to take a look at you?"

"Naw, I'll be okay. Nothing a few weeks won't heal. Excuse me, I'm going to say goodbye to Tenika."

I went to the van, which was missing a window after the shootout. I leaned through the opening and offered her my hand. "Looks like this is goodbye."

Tenika bumped her fist against mine, a gesture that served for both Renegade greetings and farewells. "Thanks for coming. I owe you one, mortal."

There was teasing in her voice, so I knew the "mortal" wasn't meant to offend, but for a stark moment, I wished my mortality could be otherwise. "Only one?"

"Or two. Just let me know." She gave me a number scrawled on a piece of map she'd torn from someplace. "My direct line. Come see us sometime in New York."

"It might be a while. We have some rebuilding to do after the last attack."

Her face sobered. "We all do."

"I know." She and her group were still recovering from the betrayal of one of our own that had caused Lorrie's death and led to the murder and capture of many Renegades. The same man had been responsible for my captivity. But Renegades didn't leave people behind, and we would find them as they had found me.

"We'll bring them home," I said.

She nodded. "I'll be heading back tomorrow. Maybe when these guys"—she jerked her head to the rear of the van where the unconscious Emporium agents were stacked like so much firewood—"wake up, they'll give us some new leads." Her dark eyes held mine for another long second, and I knew she felt a deep responsibility for the people she'd lost. She wasn't the only one. Maybe all survivors felt that way.

I didn't have the keys to Marisa's motorbike, so I enjoyed a long, humid walk back to the plane, using the time to report in to Ava. I arrived at the makeshift airport as the sun finally broke through the trees of the jungle. There were no signs of vehicles or lights in the small building across the expanse of dirt, which told me César and Diego Molina hadn't returned. It was just as well. I wasn't too happy with either of them after what they'd allowed Marisa to suffer while in their household. As the men in her life, they should have protected her. I would have died before I'd let my sister Erin endure what she had. They would return eventually, I had no doubt, as soon as they heard that these particular bandits were no longer a problem.

Maybe Marisa would even let them visit her eventually. I couldn't help smiling as I thought about her. I didn't doubt that she'd find someone else to love. She was that kind of woman. I envied the guy, whoever he was.

After double-checking the lock on the plane's door, I downed some rations, gulped water and a few pain killers, then fell across three seats and let myself drop into oblivion.

The next thing I knew, my phone was ringing. I groped for it and pressed it to my ear. "Hello?"

"On our way back," Erin said. "Emporium's probably not too far behind. Get the plane ready."

My watch said it was already seven that evening, so outside the plane it'd be dark. "What's your ETA?"

"Twenty minutes tops."

"I'll be ready. But we'll have to touch down for fuel in Mexico again. We're running low, and the fuel here didn't come through as planned."

"Guess we'll make do. Thanks." My sister sounded exhausted. Whatever they'd gone through apparently hadn't been easy.

After a quick preflight check, I had time to swallow more pain killers, rub some of the dry blood from my head, change into a fresh shirt, and pull on a baseball cap. The mirror showed a split lip and a nasty bruise on my cheek, but they couldn't see the bandage on my arm or the huge bruises forming on my chest and stomach. In all I didn't look too bad. No use in causing my siblings alarm. If I kept a low enough profile and didn't move too stiffly, they wouldn't guess how terribly my body ached.

Of course, with Erin, I'd also have to watch my thoughts. She wouldn't delve into my private ones without permission, but if my thoughts shouted pain, she'd easily pick up on it. With a little luck and repeated dosages of pain killer, she might never learn how close it had been.

My hopes of sliding completely under the radar were upset the moment my sister arrived. Erin's face was dirty and cut, her blond hair matted, and her gray eyes exhausted, but her concern for me was immediate. "What happened to you?" she asked as she practically fell from the Pinz—which was short for Pinzgauer, an old European army vehicle that roughly resembled a Humvee.

I walked slowly toward her, purposely clamping down on any thoughts. "Had a little run-in with some local bandits. Tried to steal our plane. Apparently, they were upset about some bad deal they made with the owners here and wanted retribution. But we held them off." I cracked a grin. "I did have to take the guy's sister hostage to make them fight with me, but it worked out."

"You'll have to tell us all about it." She linked her arm around my neck so I could help her up the steps and into the plane. I tried not to wince, failing miserably, and the fact that she didn't notice told me how taxing the day had been for her.

Erin wasn't the only one worse for wear. Our newest employee, Benito Hernández—a mortal like me—was seriously wounded, and Ritter, who was covered in blood, was carrying him. Our healer, Dimitri Sidorov, who claimed over a thousand years of life, hovered next to him with a worried expression.

Looks like we all had stories to tell, but for now I needed to get us into the air. Home to Stella.

The plane had been in flight thirty minutes when broad-shouldered Dimitri came into the cockpit where my little brother, Jace, was asking me questions about flying. Now that Jace knew he had two thousand years to live, he planned to take time to learn a little about everything. Normally, I didn't mind, but today his exuberance was exhausting.

"May I have a moment with Chris?" Dimitri asked.

"Sure." Jace exited the cockpit, curiosity showing on his face.

"What's up?" I asked Dimitri. "Is Benito okay?"

"He's tough. He's going to make it."

I sighed with relief. Jace had told me that Dimitri and the others hadn't been able to save the scientists, but Benito had been instrumental in securing a thumb drive, which we believed held the cure for Bronson, and losing him would have made everything much worse.

Dimitri drew up behind me and placed his hands on my shoulders. "Lean forward."

I grunted with the effort. "How did you know?"

"I mostly guessed after talking to Ava about your report. But I can see you're in pain."

"Don't tell Erin."

He laughed. "Yeah. Not going to do that. She'd want you tied up in bubble wrap until, well, forever. Good thing she's too exhausted to be more suspicious." He closed his eyes as his hand roamed over my chest and stomach. It could have felt weird having another man touch me that way when I was definitely heterosexual, but I knew he healed best by touch, and I was in too much pain to object. Besides, he was Erin's biological father, so he was family in more ways than our Renegade connection.

"Your ribs aren't broken," Dimitri said. "However, they are very bruised. I've done what I can to ease the pain and hurry the healing, but they'll still be sore for a few days."

"Thanks." I was already feeling better.

Finally, he pulled off my cap and began checking my head. "Do you have this thing on autopilot? Because you need stitches. It's going to hurt a bit."

"Guess I'll have to get used to pain."

"Guess so." Did he sound proud? I wasn't sure. But with my own parents out of the daily picture because of the danger the Emporium posed, I did look to him for guidance. If Ava was the leader and mother of our Renegade cell, Dimitri was the father.

I'd had stitches before and Dimitri had been underestimating his gentleness, or maybe his ability as a healer dampened the pain. I managed to endure his ministrations without making a fool of myself or causing the plane to drop from the sky. In fact, by the time he left the cockpit, my overall pain had dipped to a level that the pain killer could handle. I didn't even mind when Jace returned with his incessant, eager questions. He was alive and that was enough.

We had barely entered US airspace some hours later when Ava contacted us with the news: Bronson was dead.

Her words slammed into me, and for a long moment I struggled for breath. All the work, the hurry, the sacrifice. The deaths of the scientists. It had all been for nothing.

We were too late.

WE ARRIVED IN PORTLAND WITH THE MORNING SUN, WHOSE light did nothing to remove the heaviness from my chest. While I dealt with arrangements for the plane after landing, the others went to Stella's apartment, which we were using as a temporary safe house until we moved to the new place in San Diego. I also had to meet the ambulance that came for Benito, and by the time I arrived at Stella's, the place was a hive of activity.

"This location has been compromised," Erin told me, appearing from the back of the moving truck outside the apartment. "But guess what? There was information on that thumb drive we brought back about Tenika's missing people. We know where they're being held!"

A weight lifted from my shoulders. Maybe Mexico hadn't been a total bust after all.

"We're leaving as soon as possible," Ritter added. He jumped down from the truck and turned to offer Erin a hand. At over two hundred and seventy years old, he sometimes had the distinct manners of an old-world gentleman, though I usually didn't see even a glimpse of that because he was otherwise so deadly—a killing machine, really. But I'd noticed that Erin brought out this other side of him, the gallantry from a time long forgotten by most of us.

Erin ignored his hand and came down the ramp, but the look she tossed him at the bottom told me she had been aware of him and wasn't ready to accept him completely. Something had happened between them in Mexico. I hoped it was good.

Ava came from Stella's third-floor apartment, her feet making noise on the outside metal staircase as she descended. I turned to her. "I just need to see my kids, then I'll go back to the airport to get the plane ready for the flight."

Ava shook her head. "No. Cort will take us in the smaller plane. He's skilled enough for that. I want you to load the essentials and take them to the house in San Diego. George and Charles will go with you. I'll arrange for Benito to join you once he's out of the hospital. You might want to send the kids to your parents for a while until you're sure the new place is secure." Her lips tightened. "I want it to be a veritable fortress when you're finished."

Fortress. It reminded me of two days earlier when Erin had begged me to take the kids and leave the Renegades. I'd told her that separating them from those they loved wasn't the answer, but rather making sure it never happened again. I was just the man for creating the fortress. My children could be killed, so I had the most to lose.

However, it didn't escape me that Ava was sending

the mortals with me, while the Unbounded would be going to what would likely be another bloodbath with the Emporium.

"Please, Chris," Ava said, her hand going out to mine. "We must free our people, but after losing Stella's baby and Gaven like that and"—she swallowed hard—"almost losing the kids, and now Bronson, we need a refuge to come home to. Right now we really need everyone to be safe."

The mortals to be safe, she meant.

I looked into her face, with her steel gray eyes so like my own and Erin's. This fourth great-grandmother, who was basically my physical age, had lost so much over the years, and the mortals in our cell were particularly vulnerable, regardless of any black ops experience. I understood Ava wanting to limit further loss. Losing Lorrie had made me seek revenge, but if I lost one of my children now, there wouldn't be anything of me left, and losing more Renegades in the near future might be the beginning of the end in our struggle against the Emporium.

"Okay," I said. "I'll make that house a fortress. You watch over Erin and Jace."

She nodded. "With my life."

I knew she meant it. And not only her, but Ritter, Stella, and the others. "What about Marco?" I asked. Marco Collins was the one mortal employee she hadn't mentioned, one who'd served with Gaven in black ops and who would mourn him the most.

"I'll take him with us. He needs the distraction, and we'll need someone for legwork."

I knew that meant she would keep an eye on him and make sure he was far from any real action. Marco would hate that if he knew, but being left behind would annoy him more. I nodded and started up the stairs.

"We're putting most of the essentials in the vehicles for you to take to the plane," Ava called after me. "We've also hired a driver for the moving truck. We need to be out of here in the next thirty minutes."

I nodded. "I'm ready." We'd lost most of our belongings when we'd torched the old safe house after the Emporium raid, so I didn't have anything to pack that wasn't already in my Jeep. The kids didn't have much left either, except what Ava and the others had pulled from their rooms before starting the fire to cover all the damage. Our concern had focused on electronics, not on stuff we could easily replace.

I went into the apartment, through the front room, and down the hallway to the closet. Inside the closet was a hidden door leading to a room where my children had been when I'd said goodbye before going to Mexico. I wanted to hold them and see for myself that they were all right. But I'd gone only halfway down the hall when they emerged from what had been Bronson's bedroom.

"Dad, you're back!" Kathy exclaimed, throwing herself at me, her blond hair swinging around her face. For an instant, pain shot through me at her resemblance to her mother, but the emotion passed as her arms wrapped around my neck. She was only twelve, but it felt like she'd grown an inch in just the two days I'd been away.

"Bronson's dead!" Spencer hugged my waist, and I dropped to take them both in my arms, nodding a greeting at Charles, the husky man who was watching over them.

"I know, son. But it's going to be okay." My arms tightened as gratitude choked me. I was so grateful to be holding them again.

"We're leaving soon," Charles said, his wide chin set. Sadness radiated from his brown eyes—eyes that looked dark against the paleness of his face. I knew he missed Gaven almost as much as Marco did.

"Look, you two need to get ready," I told the kids. "Charles and I are taking you to Grandma and Grandpa's for a few weeks until we get the security system installed in our new place."

"Ava showed us a picture," Kathy said. "It's huge. A mansion!"

"She says we can have a playroom with a climbing wall," Spencer added. "Can we, Dad?"

"Sure."

"Anyway, we're already packed," Kathy said. "We didn't have much from the old house."

Spencer pulled back, his freckled nose wrinkling and reminding me faintly of Marisa. "Are we going to get new clothes again?"

"Yeah, bud, we are." Reluctantly, I released them and

stood. "If you'll stay with them a bit longer," I said to Charles, "I'll meet you guys in the Jeep. We can drive them to my parents and then meet George at the plane." Though my parents lived in Portland, it'd take a couple hours to follow the precautions necessary for turning over the children. The Emporium had eyes everywhere these days. We'd need Charles for backup.

Charles shook his head. "We're having a brief service for Bronson and Gaven at the mortuary in about an hour, before the others leave for New York. Gaven's family will hold their own service in Alabama, so he'll be sent there afterward."

"Yeah, we need to be there," Kathy said, blinking back tears.

Mentally I began adjusting my plan. The service was a good idea, and I was glad someone had thought of it. I needed closure as much as anyone. "Okay, then. After the service."

"We'll meet you outside," Charles said.

I nodded. "Be sure to take Max," I told the kids. We couldn't forget the dog. He'd love to visit my parents, who were his original owners.

I watched them go before stepping into Bronson's room where his body lay, still and gray-looking. Stella sat in the chair by the bed, appearing almost completely well instead of half dead the way I'd had to leave her. I clamped down to stop the relief; after all, she was Unbounded and healing was expected. But I knew some wounds couldn't be seen.

She was even more beautiful than I remembered. Her shoulder-length black hair was smooth and glossy, her heart-shaped face, sculptured eyebrows, and flawless olive skin perfect. Her Asian heritage lent a kind of mystery to her features that begged me to learn more. I wanted to take her in my arms and protect her.

She looked up and saw me, her mouth curving in a sad smile that I was ashamed to admit did more for me than Marisa's passionate kiss. "They say it helps to say goodbye. I hope it's okay that I let the children see him this way."

"Of course." I trusted her. She'd saved their lives, and in a way that meant they were hers now. If I'd known Bronson's body was still in here, I probably would have talked to them about it, but I suspected Stella and Ava already had—and better than I could have. They both knew more about death than I did, despite my recent loss.

She stood, leaning over to stroke Bronson's pale cheek before straightening and facing me again. "You've probably heard about the service, but I need to stay until Bronson's properly buried. In a few days, I'll join the others in New York."

"You can't stay here. It's too dangerous."

"I know. I'll find a hotel. I'm not sure where I want to bury him. Maybe you can fly him somewhere for me? Maybe to San Diego?"

I would deny her nothing. "If that's what you want."

She nodded.

I stepped closer, then took her into my arms the way I'd wanted to since walking into that room. Well, not exactly the way that I wanted, but it was all I'd ever have. "Stella, I wanted to tell you before we left, but you were still . . ." *Unconscious.* "Asleep. I—you . . . you saved my children. You could have made so many other choices, but you didn't, and I can never, ever repay you for that. Thank you." I didn't mention her lost baby because I could feel it there between us, heavy and aching. I wasn't sure what I would do if she started crying. I wanted smooth her hair, to caress her face, to take away her pain. Love it away. As if that could do it. I knew it wouldn't begin to come close.

She pulled back. "Oh, Chris, I am so glad I was there for them. Whatever happened, I don't regret that. I love those kids, and I know how you feel about them. They are the reason for this fight. I would never let anything happen to them, if I could help it. I don't regret what I did."

"I know." But the cost had been higher than any of us would have wanted her to pay.

"Come with me," I said gently. "Ava will take care of Bronson until the service. We'll go for a drive with the kids before we head over." With the apartment location compromised, I wanted to be sure Stella was out of here long before the Emporium agents arrived. And they would come. It was only a matter of time.

Mutely, she nodded and let me turn her toward the door.

I took one last look over my shoulder at Bronson. I'd liked him, the retired electronics engineer with a steady hand, who'd removed more bullets from Stella and her friends than most mortal doctors. At seventy he looked more like Stella's father or even grandfather than her husband. I knew he'd been married once before meeting her and had two grown children. He'd lived a good life, if short by Unbounded standards. But he looked at peace. Maybe he hadn't been all that unhappy to leave before age separated him even more from the woman he loved.

*Goodbye, old man,* I thought. *We'll take care of her.*

Ava met us in the hallway with Ritter and Dimitri, who hurried into the room and picked up Bronson. "We have to leave right now. Make sure you're armed."

# CHAPTER 11

THREE DAYS LATER I WAS STILL IN PORTLAND—AND STILL ON edge, wondering where the Emporium would strike next. Stella had changed her mind about transporting Bronson to San Diego, mostly because his adult children lived in Washington and driving to Portland for a proper funeral and subsequent visits to his grave would be easier for their families than traveling clear to Southern California. I was glad because I thought having Bronson buried in San Diego, so near our new safe house, might cause Stella more pain.

I stayed with her at first because there was no one else. Then Ava called to let me know the New York Renegade cell had intercepted an encrypted message from the Emporium that mentioned pending activity in our area, and there was no way I was leaving her alone after that. I didn't tell Stella, but I became even more vigilant. I kept

Charles with us and sent George ahead to San Diego to meet with the contractor who was doing the house renovations.

We'd spent the first day making funeral preparations for Bronson. Or rather, Stella made the preparations. Charles and I shared her hotel suite, but we'd consumed most of the time pouring over security options for the house while she'd been making phone calls, hotel arrangements for Bronson's family, and talking to the mortuary. Charles also watched old *Star Trek* reruns, which soon began to make me wish I could beam him out of there. But he was a good pizza buddy, and we consumed far more than our share. He preferred the more exotic kind, like those with kelp and shrimp and white sauce, while I loved pepperoni and sausage.

Even preoccupied as she was with Bronson, Stella did more research than we did into our future security arrangements, vetting companies we might employ to help us create our fortress. I knew she would also ensure that whatever company we chose didn't retain enough information about us in their files to ever betray us to the Emporium.

Dealing with our immediate security problems kept Stella's brain occupied at a time when she desperately needed it. She'd be talking funeral arrangements with the mortuary, and at the same time sending me background checks on all the employees at a security company, complete with lists of their loved ones and associates and charity donations. At the same time, I'd receive a dozen new articles from her on the latest in security options. Having a technopath around had its advantages, but deep down I admitted that her capabilities served mostly to emphasize the gap between us. That was when I wished I could beam myself elsewhere.

Except for when Stella would melt into tears in my arms. Then I was glad that I was with her—whatever it might cost me.

On the third morning, we held the small funeral, consisting only of Bronson's children and grandchildren, four golf buddies, a dozen people from the church he'd attended, and two men he'd served with in the Navy as a teen. Stella dressed the part of the grieving widow in a trim black suit and hat. It reminded me of something worn at funerals fifty years ago minus the veil across the eyes.

She'd Changed early, at twenty-eight, almost two centuries ago, which put her physically at thirty-two, but today she'd directed her nanites to change her appearance, faintly aging her skin so Bronson's children wouldn't wonder at her youth. "Black gloves and my half-Japanese heritage should take care of the rest," she said.

I knew some technopaths could use nanites to slightly alter their faces, and that Stella had enhanced her appearance for years. She claimed that if Cort created faster, more intricate nanites, she might be able to age far more convincingly, but as it was, the nanites had severe limitations, made more difficult by the Unbounded metabolism that worked hard to put everything back the way it was supposed to be. Even with the aging, she was still beautiful. Seeing her as she might look in a thousand years brought a lump to my throat that didn't leave for the whole service.

I told myself I was only worried about the Emporium crashing our party.

We both wore bulletproof vests under our clothes, which wasn't nearly the problem it was in the jungle because Oregon was cold and the added heat welcome. Our coats hid any unseemly bulk. But there were no problems at the funeral and no interruptions at the cemetery.

Finally it was over, and we headed for the airport, checking for a possible tail as we always did. Charles was meeting me at our plane with a few more supplies, and Stella was taking a commercial flight to New York. I was tempted to go with her, but I had my orders from Ava, and I was anxious to get to work so that I could be reunited with my children. Our Renegades were depending on me to create a safe haven, a fortress, and that's what I'd do. I'd already directed the contractor to fill the walls with more cables than my security plans would ever need, but I was feeling pressure to get there and make sure it was done right.

There was a little time before her flight, so Stella dropped me off at the sprawling corrugated metal hangar that we rented and shared with a half dozen other companies. I still had preflight checks and clearances to undergo before I followed through on my filed flight plan, and she'd most likely be in the air on her flight to New York before I took off.

I pushed open the car door, planning to wave a casual goodbye, but Stella killed the engine. I raised my eyebrows. "I'll come in to say goodbye to Charles," she explained. Already her face had returned to normal.

"He should be here," I said, looking around. "But I don't see the rental car. Unless he changed plans, the car company was supposed to pick it up here."

"I can wait."

I didn't remind her that she'd said goodbye to Charles before the funeral, which he'd attended, though he hadn't gone to the gravesite itself with us afterward. I had the feeling her coming into the hangar wasn't about Charles at all, but I couldn't exactly call her on it. Maybe she just liked planes. That I could understand.

I unlocked the hangar and deactivated the alarm. Stella followed me inside a lobby that was really more of a shared hangout where pilots and businessmen would rest between flights when there wasn't time to go home. We had vending machines, a television, couches, and restrooms. It was better than a lot of hangars I'd worked out of. I could tell no one was here at the moment because the heat was off. I reset the alarm.

Opening the door to the main part of the hangar, I turned on some lights that were still far too dim in the vast space. We had more light coming from the windows in the hangar doors themselves than from the artificial lights, even on this cloudy, winter day.

The door closed behind us as we started down the lines of planes, each one backed in like a car in a garage. The hangar didn't have many frills, but we each had a small office and a large wheeled cart to store tools. We also shared a maintenance guy who worked on the planes and went up in the overhead rafters to change the lights. The smell of engines and planes reminded me of my first job in a garage when I was in high school. It was the year the flying bug had bitten deeply after I'd gone up in a small two-seater with one of the clients.

A couple of the newer planes were state-of-the-art corporate jets, and I'd salivated over them more than once or twice. I'd even flown a few on occasions in the two months we'd been here, pinch-hitting for their pilots or riding copilot.

"Doesn't look like Charles is here yet," I said as we reached our plane. Door was shut, no lights inside. "I'd better open the hangar door. Got a lot to do before takeoff."

"Chris, wait." Stella's hand fell on my arm. "Look, thank you for staying here so long to help me with everything. You really didn't have to."

"I needed to research security systems anyway. And, let's face it, you helped me more than I did you."

Her hand didn't leave my arm, and I became acutely aware of how isolated we were alone inside this remote hangar, separated by only the sleeve of my jacket.

"It was the least I could do," she said. "The house in

San Diego is beautiful, but it's going to need heavy renovations to become what we need."

"My plan is to have it done in four weeks. Or most of it," I said. "Thanks to Ava pulling strings with that big contractor. I'm meeting the security company there tonight."

"No more running." Stella was keeping up the conversation, but her eyes were far away. "It'll be good to have a permanent place."

There was also danger in staying put, but she was right that it felt good. "I'll make it safe."

I'd made a similar promise, though not in so many words, to Lorrie all those years ago when we married. No way could I guess that fourteen years and two children later we would be facing an Emporium hit team, or that Lorrie would step in the way of a bullet meant for me. None of that had been in my plans. Neither could I have dreamed of what Stella would sacrifice for my children. This time I was going to make sure no one got to my family or any of the Renegades.

Something of my thoughts must have shown in my face because Stella said quietly, "It's not your fault."

Her touch still burned through my sleeve. "I know."

Her mouth parted, her tongue wetting her lips. She seemed about to say more but suddenly leaned over to hug me, burying her face in my chest and making it difficult for me to think about anything except how wonderful her hair smelled and how right she felt in my arms. I'd held her quite a few times this way in the past few days, and if I was honest with myself, I didn't know how much more I could take without doing something to scare her away. She was so alive and yet so vulnerable. I didn't trust myself as much as she seemed to.

However, I did understand her—the yearning for children, the cold, gaping emptiness that had once been filled with warmth and love, and most of all the guilt for being the one left alive. Her nearness made me forget all of that, made me forget everything but the furious pounding of my heart. She had to notice its throbbing with her cheek pressed tightly against my chest. I let my hand creep up to touch her silky hair.

"Look, Chris," she said softly without meeting my gaze, "I want a baby. I've already lived more than three lifetimes, and I don't want to wait any longer." A small hiccup marred the last words. She drew back and looked up into my eyes. "I delayed too long with Bronson. I have to live with that, and with him being gone forever, but I can still have a baby, if you'll help me."

Emotions tumbled through me. My body felt alive with them, but my brain warned caution. "What are you saying?"

"This." She put her arms around my neck, stretching up to meet me. I felt helpless as her lips touched mine. Then I was kissing her, pulling her closer, ignoring the twinge in my split lip that wasn't quite healed. If it had been any other woman, wanting her in this way would have made me feel disloyal to Lorrie, but it was Stella, who'd saved our babies' lives, who'd lost so much with Bronson's death. I wanted her. I'd be crazy not to.

Except somewhere in the part of me that was still sane, I knew this wasn't Stella talking. Maybe it would be some day, but not now. Not with Bronson so newly gone and her baby so recently lost. Unbounded or not, she needed more time. Maybe I did too.

I pulled backward until I hit the door to our office, but she followed me, not letting me go. She was soft, so full of life! I wanted her more than I'd probably wanted anything in a long time. My body screamed in protest at my inaction.

*It's too soon.*

Her beautiful eyes held mine, begging for my agreement. I had to at least try to prevent us from making this mistake. For her sake.

I put my hands on her shoulders, holding her away from me. "Stella," I said with a strained voice I barely recognized as my own. "I know you're missing Bronson, but you're not thinking straight right now. I know because I went through the same thing when I lost Lorrie, and I—"

She chopped at my arms, forcing them from her shoulders. "You don't *know* anything!" Tears started down her face. "I watched Bronson grow old. I watched him change from the vital man I married to an old, sick stranger, who had no interest in going on trips or going hiking or even leaving the house. No interest in sex. I loved him so much, but the Bronson who died wasn't the man I fell in love with—and I couldn't grow old with him or change with him."

She was crying full force now and tearing my heart in two with her anguish. Her pain was deep and raw. "It wasn't fair. It's just not fair!" Again her face buried in my chest, and I held on to her, tears pricking my own eyes. There was nothing I could do but hold her.

After a long time the storm abated. "Yes," she said with another little hiccup, pulling away once more to look into my face. "I miss Bronson, but I miss the man I fell in love with, not the old man who went on without me. I miss feeling his body against mine. I miss being wanted more than food or work or the newest television show. I miss the nights we didn't sleep because we couldn't get enough of each other. I miss camping under the stars, traveling all over the world. I miss it all!" She paused and took a deep breath. "But none of that's new. I've missed him for years. All I could do was to cling to what we had left."

She slumped dejectedly. Wanting to comfort her, I pulled her tightly against me. Her face lifted to mine, her lips beckoning to be kissed, and I wanted more than anything to do that. My thin control vanished, and my lips met hers. This was where I wanted to be, and though I knew I shouldn't be doing this, I didn't know how to stop myself. Her lips parted and I tasted her passion. It took me three tries before I could pull away enough to clear my throat and speak.

"Oh, Stella," I whispered, "you have no idea how much I want you right now. But I won't take advantage of your grief." There, the words were out. I knew I might regret them for the rest of my life. I also knew that if she kissed me again, all my brave words would mean absolutely nothing.

Silence fell for a long moment as she searched my face. When she spoke, her words were calmer. "Then just give me a baby." She didn't add that I owed her, but we both knew I did. She'd saved my children, and if I gave her a hundred babies, it would never be enough to make up for the one she'd lost.

I opened my mouth to speak, though I didn't know what would come out. Whatever the words, they were lost as the sound of gunfire broke through the air, shattering my indecision.

I grabbed Stella and dived with her behind the metal tool station.

# CHAPTER 12

I HADN'T BEEN CAREFUL ABOUT OUR TRAJECTORY, AND I landed on my back, with Stella on top of me. Despite Dimitri's earlier ministrations, pain shot through my ribs. I gritted my teeth and reached for my gun.

Stella already had her pistol out. She eased off me, peering around the tool station. "I don't think they're firing at us," she whispered. "Did that come from the lobby?"

"I think so. They must be firing at Charles. Probably attacked him after he entered but before he reset the alarm because I don't hear it. But they'll know someone else is here because of the lights and the car. Look, I'll be right back. Cover me." I stood and darted to the next tool cart and then to a group of light switches. They had them embedded periodically along the wall so that we wouldn't have to go all the way to the lobby doors to shut them on or off. I turned off all four circuits that lit the vast space and returned to Stella.

"How did they find us?" This close I could see her eyes widen with a possibility. "You don't think it was the funeral, do you? Maybe they suspected that Bronson was linked to the Renegades. I tried to keep him away from that side of my life, but they could have identified him and tracked us from the graveyard." She paused, and when she spoke again, her voice sounded panicked. "You don't think they followed Bronson's kids, do you? I'd never forgive myself if—"

"No," I said more gruffly than I intended. "They would have attacked us at the mortuary or at the cemetery. We were there by ourselves. Would have been easy to pick us off. No, I think they've been watching this hangar. Must have traced the flight from Mexico." That meant César and Diego had returned to their little house by the makeshift runway. I hoped for Marisa's sake that the Emporium had left them alive.

"I should have created new numbers and papers," Stella said. "I always do that when there's any possibility of being traced."

"We didn't know there was a need."

My words didn't fool her. All the excuses in the world wouldn't be enough. "I should have done it."

"Must be Marco they're firing at."

"We have to help him."

"They won't kill him. Not until they get inside the plane or find us."

"I hope you're right."

So did I.

I took the lead. After two centuries of training, Stella was more experienced, and in a fair fight, she'd hand me my head on a platter, but this hangar was my domain. Problem was that we kept a fairly uncluttered place, and besides the wheeled tool stations, and the planes themselves, there wasn't much to hide us. Inside the office, we'd be sitting ducks. I opened the tool cart and took out the largest wire cutters I had. "Take whatever you think you might need. You have enough ammo?"

"Two extra magazines." She was putting on her silencer as she spoke. "Never leave home without them."

"Sounds like Ritter."

"I learned from the best. Wish I had an assault rifle, though."

I was glad to hear the panic was gone from her voice. In fact, she sounded almost excited. Yet I didn't like the idea of her in another confrontation so soon.

I motioned to the ladder next to the office door. "I'm going up and over the catwalks they use to change the lights. I'll see if I can drop down behind them when they come in, or maybe shoot them from above. I might be able to cut the wiring to the lights. Darkness is in our favor, especially if they're used to the light outside."

"I'll cover you."

She meant in case they came in while I was on my way up, but I didn't intend to let that happen. I hurried up the ladder, skipping two rungs with every step. It was a long, long way up, but the catwalks came quicker than expected. As I reached the top, I spied the first of the electrical circuits and snipped the wires, then hurried along the catwalk to the next. A thin but sturdy piece of metal formed a halfway decent handrail on one side of the catwalk, but it was a good thing I didn't share my sister's acrophobia—something her Change hadn't fixed.

I'd only snipped two circuits when the door from the lobby slammed opened. "Where are the damn lights?" someone growled.

I sprinted to the wiring of the third circuit and cut it a half second before the lights came on in the farthermost section. Well, I obviously wouldn't make it to that circuit in time, but at least I'd taken out three of the four.

I lay flat on the catwalk, knowing they would soon be looking instinctively upward as they continued to flip the switches, trying to get the other circuits on.

"That's it?" one of the men below growled. "No more lights?"

"It's a hangar," Charles said, "not a hotel."

"Shut up."

The failing lights should let Charles know I was here, but I hoped that knowledge wouldn't make him over-confident. It was still us versus six Emporium agents, all dressed in black, carrying pistols and wearing sword sheaths. Two of them held assault rifles. Definitely an Emporium hit team. I tried to match their faces with the files we had on known Emporium agents, but nothing was coming to me. I didn't know how many were

Unbounded and how many might be mortal soldiers, but I had to assume the worst. That meant six combatants who wouldn't really die unless I dismembered them.

Of course to get that far, I first had to immobilize them. Or temporarily kill them.

Maybe it was better that I didn't know which might be Unbounded and which were mortal. Knowing might make me hesitate.

"You two find the lights," said a big Latino, who seemed to be in charge. "Meet us at the plane."

I stayed motionless as they left the entrance and started down the line of planes. I couldn't risk them seeing me in the dim light. But two staying behind was good because my plane was parked on the very end of the row, and the others would soon be far enough away for me to act safely.

Three men and one woman took off down the line of planes with Charles, while the man and woman who stayed behind continued flipping light switches and staring above them. Nothing to do but wait until they grew bored and tried something else.

"I'll go see if there's a circuit breaker out there," the man finally said, opening the door to the lobby.

"Okay, but keep your eyes open. More Renegade scum could be arriving."

"Got babe here to protect us." He patted his assault rifle and disappeared through the door. The woman took a tool from her belt and began to unscrew the metal plate behind the light switches.

The others were out of my sight, though I could hear their footsteps echoing in the hangar. I eased to my feet and tried to move soundlessly along the catwalk until I was positioned above the woman.

*Wait,* I told myself as I knelt and took careful aim. I had to make sure her companions were far enough away that they wouldn't hear the soft whoosh of my silenced bullet or notice her go down. I hoped with the positioning of the tool carts near each plane, they might not see her body even if they looked this way. My rifle and a scope would be better for this job, but the nine mil would have to do. The hit team were most likely wearing some kind of body armor, so I had to try for a headshot.

*Now.* I pulled the trigger. *Whoosh!* She slumped almost immediately, her head making a cracking sound on the cement when she fell. Blood and brains spread over the ground around her head, leaking from her skull, though I couldn't see exactly where I'd hit her.

I stood and moved as fast as I could to the space above the entry. I was in the light now, if anyone had been there to look up, but the Emporium agent was beyond seeing anything. Positioning myself directly above the lobby door, I waited. How long would it take the male agent to discover the breaker wasn't in there? Not long, I hoped. There were no gunshots coming from the other side of the hangar, but I itched to get back there. My own success had proven that the sound of silenced shots didn't carry that far.

The door opened almost before I was ready. My hands

waved into position as the man came through. "I can't find—Sasha!"

He'd taken only two steps toward his fallen companion when I fired. This time two shots, because I wasn't sure of my aim and he was moving. The first hit him near the top of his head and the second embedded in the base of his skull. I felt a momentary triumph, until the urge to vomit nearly made me fall from the catwalk.

*Don't think about it. Not yet.*

Ritter had been right about all those target practices paying off, but he hadn't told me about this revulsion. Maybe because he'd lost that in the years he'd sought revenge for his own family's deaths.

*Stella. Charles.* I had to think of them now.

I debated briefly over whether or not I should climb down the ladder and hide the bodies, but there was no way to clean the blood from the cement, so that was rather pointless. Better that I go help the others. Pulling myself together, I started again along the catwalk.

Two down, four to go. The odds had just gotten slightly better.

I had the hangar divided mentally into four parts, corresponding with the electric circuits. I passed gratefully from the first and into the second, going slower now, treading with caution. I'd almost reached the third section when light footsteps below alerted me to someone coming back this way. I paused and waited. An Emporium agent came into view below, walking with exaggerated steps, his hands holding an assault rifle.

He was white and young, probably young enough that he didn't know if he'd Change and become Unbounded or if he'd serve the Emporium as a second class citizen for the rest of his mortal life.

I thought of my brother Jace, newly Changed and, like Stella, younger than most Unbounded. Maybe this man had Changed early too. It didn't matter, though. The hit man below supported the Emporium and there was simply no excuse for coming here with that assault rifle.

Heart banging inside my chest, I waited to fire until he stepped over to the wall and the light switches. My bullet hit him in the head, and he fell against the wall and slid down slowly without a sound. I waited only to be sure he wasn't moving.

Three against three now.

I began moving faster, experiencing a strange urgency. It was a miracle I didn't fall as I tore through the third section. *Slow down,* I told myself. Ritter had emphasized repeatedly the importance of waiting every bit as much as the will to attack, and I had come too far to give up the advantage I held up here in the dark. So far, Ritter's training had not failed me. I popped out my old magazine, still more than half full, and slid in a new one. Twelve rounds in all.

A loud shout farther ahead and to my right urged me on. The sound came from below somewhere near where my plane or the one next to it was parked. I hurried forward as quickly as I could, reaching one of the intersections of the catwalk where it shot out over each parking space.

Below, I heard a flurry of whooshing sounds I'd been dreading. Silenced bullets.

I reached the halfway point on the catwalk where it again intersected another line that paralleled the first. Nothing was under me except a plane, and I couldn't yet see beyond it to my own. I pushed forward along the catwalk. Finally, I caught sight of an Emporium agent standing near my plane, her gun pressed into Charles's back.

"Who's shooting at us!" she demanded, shielding her body between Charles and the stairs to my plane.

"Maybe the IRS? Did you pay your taxes?"

I never knew Charles to be such a wise guy. Maybe all that kelp on his pizza was having a strange side effect.

"I'm going to enjoy killing you," the Unbounded said. "Now get up these stairs and open the door, or I'm going to start shooting off your fingers one by one." The way she said it was more of a promise than anything else, and I suspected that without intervention, Charles would lose all his fingers even if he did open the door. I contemplated shooting the woman as I had the others, but she was too close to my plane. Almost under it now. The angle was poor enough that to hit her, the bullet might first have to go through Charles.

I had only seconds to decide. In the dark, I spied two shadows taking cover behind the next plane's tool station. A flash of a gun going off showed me Stella was firing from behind our own station, the one we'd hidden behind earlier. I wanted to backtrack across the catwalk and drop in behind the other Emporium agents to help Stella, and I knew Charles would insist on it if he had a choice, but my doing so would leave him vulnerable. She was Unbounded; he was not. I knew where my duty lay. I couldn't let my feelings for Stella fool me into thinking she'd thank me for sacrificing Charles. She could hold her own.

"What's the code?" screamed the Emporium woman. "You know what? If you aren't going to help, I'll just kill you right here!" She dug her gun into Charles's neck. "Tell me the code and I might let you live."

Charles shook his head. "Go ahead, shoot me. I'm dead if I let you in anyway."

In a quick motion, she put her arm around his neck and pulled back. Charles began to choke.

I knew what I had to do.

# CHAPTER 13

HOLSTERING MY GUN, I GRABBED THE CATWALK AND EASED myself down until I was only three feet from the top of my plane. In all our training, we'd never practiced jumping from heights onto a curved surface, but how much more difficult could it be?

I let go, and my feet clunked hard against the plane. I swore silently, struggling to retain my balance. No dice. I slid off the plane, landing feet first on the ground, remembering at the last second not to lock my knees but to bend and roll. I came up ready to shoot, hoping my rolling angle was enough to give me a line to the woman agent without Charles in the way. I fired.

They both fell, but not before the woman let off a shot that dug into the cement inches away from my head. Only the fact that I was still in motion saved my life. I fired again at the woman's slumped figure and hurried to

Charles, keeping my gun on her. Charles was out cold, but he was breathing and his windpipe seemed intact. I could see no other wounds besides a few punch marks on his face that were going to be nasty bruises in a few hours. The woman stirred and I pulled the trigger again, this time hitting her between the eyes. I stopped only to make sure she wasn't breathing.

I hurried to the end of the plane, where even in the dull light I couldn't miss the drama playing out with Stella and the remaining two Unbounded. She was swinging a large wrench at a man who blocked with a sword. Another agent lay on the ground behind the first, stunned but still moving. They'd evidently used all their extra ammo, or Stella had shot their guns from their hands.

Or not.

Even as I watched, the fallen man lifted a gun. I fired first, missing his head, but hitting him in the shoulder and causing his bullet to go wide. His second shot was better.

But so was mine, and he finally lay still.

The remaining Emporium agent had Stella by the hair, the point of his sword digging into her neck. "Shoot him!" Stella said. "Now!" Blood oozed from the front of her black skirt, a last parting gift from the man I'd just shot. I hoped he hadn't hit an artery.

"Okay," I started to take aim, my movements exaggerated.

"I'll cut off her pretty face," the agent growled.

"Hmm," I said. "Do you think you can cut her into

three before I stop you? It might be an interesting test. If you're a combat Unbounded, you might actually make it before I manage to hit you, but I don't think you can kill her and get to me, no matter how fast you are." I hoped I was right. "Next thing you know, I'll be the one using your pretty sword."

The Unbounded thought about it and then nodded. "Let me go, and I'll free her."

I met Stella's eyes, not his. "I don't think so. Say goodbye."

Stella twisted as I fired. Thankfully, she'd understood my signal. Thankfully, it was enough. The shot hit him in the throat, though I'd been aiming for his eye. Good thing Stella had moved. The last thing I wanted to explain to Ava was that I'd shot Stella and she'd be out recovering instead of flying to New York.

I rushed to Stella, grimaced at the blood seeping from her neck. "It's okay," she muttered. "It's not deep. My leg's worse."

"Lie down. I'll bandage it. Then we'll tie up these guys."

"Not here." She gritted her teeth against the pain. "They called for reinforcements when I started firing. They could be here any minute."

"Okay, but you're coming with me." She didn't argue and I knew that meant she was feeling worse than she let on. "Did you leave anything important in the car?"

"No. I only need what's in my shoulder bag over there."

I scooped up both her and the bag and ran for the plane. It took only moments to punch in the code, while Stella placed her hand on the reader. The door slid open. Ducking inside, I set her on the first row of seats, tossed her a first aid kit, and hurried back down the stairs for Charles.

"Come on, wake up," I said, gently slapping his face. That didn't work. Charles was a rather large man, so I ended up having to mostly drag him up the stairs. My ribs ached horribly by the time I finally laid him on the row of seats that faced those where I'd placed Stella. I set my backup pistol on the table between the two rows, just in case those reinforcements showed up before we were out of here.

Stella had tied a bandage around her upper leg to stem the blood flow, and now had her phone out. She'd also hung a small neural transmitter over her left ear, its metal prongs digging into her scalp. It was a smaller version of her regular headset, which was packed away and sent ahead with the others to New York. Two blinking lights on the transmitter showed it was working.

"Hacking into the airport systems now," she said. "I'll have your flight information and registration numbers changed five times and then some before we're anywhere near landing. You'll look like you came from Arkansas or somewhere in Virginia. In another two minutes, this plane will have never been anywhere near Mexico."

That was good. No way did I want more Emporium agents waiting for us in San Diego. We had measures in place to stay under the radar, from a way to change the actual physical numbers on our plane to getting through security checks with our weapons intact. Part of it involved bribes and connections with people who knew about Unbounded and the secret war being waged, but more was because of Stella's intricately designed back door into their network and her ability to manipulate and process data. She had previously created hundreds of backgrounds for this plane. It was just a matter of choosing one. Or as many as it took.

Of course the Emporium had a similar setup, which was why they had been able to find us and get this close to our hangar with weapons, but they wouldn't be able to trace us or our interference once we erased the connection to Mexico.

"Thanks," I told Stella. "While you're at it maybe you can clear us for flight a little sooner."

I hesitated at the plane door, wondering if I should go back for at least a couple of the Emporium agents, but the worry I'd heard in Stella's voice made me nix the idea. I needed to get her to safety, and that meant out of the hangar and into the sky. I hit the switch to pull the retractable stairs into place in the underbelly of the plane and sealed the door.

"I also need you to go over all the security footage for the hangar," I told Stella. "The alarm wasn't triggered, but it's possible they were here earlier and sabotaged the plane."

"I've already downloaded the footage. It'll take fifty

seconds to skim through the time since you last landed. The data connection here isn't as fast as it should be."

I grinned. "I think I can wait fifty seconds."

I headed for the cockpit, ticking off in my mind all the minimum checks I had to do before we took off. It was standard protocol to keep the plane full of fuel to speed up takeoff in an emergency, and I'd filled it after Mexico, but there were certain things I had to do before every flight. There would also be more security checks before takeoff, including making sure our weapons were secured in the specially lined compartments in the floor. I wouldn't store them until I was sure we weren't going to run into any more Emporium soldiers.

Inside the cockpit, I had an opener for one of the three hangar doors spanning the length of the hangar, but belatedly I wondered if the door was on the same circuit as the lights. I was betting not.

"Go ahead," Stella called through the open cockpit door. "We're clear on the security footage."

I began flipping levers and pushing buttons, and when the time came, the hangar door slid open, verifying my guess, though I'd already planned what it would take to splice back the electric wires and defend the hangar just in case. Finally, something had gone our way.

Twenty minutes later, we were on a runway awaiting final clearance. That we'd only had to undergo one brief physical inspection was a tribute to Stella's ability and genius. Plus, she'd already scheduled herself on another commercial flight out from San Diego. We kept emergency clothes on the plane, so she wouldn't even leave the airport.

I looked up from my readouts as a hand fell on my shoulder. Removing my headphones, I stared into Stella's face, glad she appeared less pinched after a couple of shots of curequick. "You should rest," I said, swiveling toward her.

She was still wearing the neural transmitter, but it emitted a series of flashes and then went black. "About the baby," she began.

So we were back to that. I would be lying if I said I hadn't been expecting it.

"You just saved my life," she continued. "The way I see it, you don't owe me anything. I mean that. But I'm still asking."

"Why me?" I didn't remind her that I was mortal—just like Bronson—or that she could have any number of Unbounded sperm donors who would be more likely to create a child who would grow up to have the active Unbounded gene. She knew all that far better than I did.

Her smile filled me with warmth. "Because you're a good father, and I want that for my baby, whether he's mortal or Unbounded. I want a man who will be there while he's growing up."

She paused for several heartbeats and then rushed on. "For the record, this has nothing to do with Bronson. I wanted his child because I loved him, but he already had children and knew he wouldn't be around for our baby. It never meant the same thing to him. He'd had a vasectomy before we married. He only agreed to let Dimitri heal him for my sake."

I stared into her eyes. I couldn't say no. If she wanted me to father her child, to raise and love him, I would do that gladly. I loved his mother; why wouldn't I love him? Maybe Bronson and I were both fools. Still, I liked the idea of Stella's genes and mine going on forever inside our posterity.

"Okay," I said.

Her lips parted in disbelief, filling me with desire. I struggled with myself not to stand up and start kissing her again, to lose myself in her touch.

*Give her more time.*

She started to speak, but I reached up and placed a finger on her lips. "First you're going to New York with the others to help free our people, and I'm going to get the house in San Diego ready to protect all of us, especially my children. When you get back, if you still want to, we'll start this baby."

The happiness in her eyes made me catch my breath, but I forced myself to continue because I'd regained enough control to remember that she needed more than just a baby. "We'll create him or her with all the genetic options we have available. And, yes, that means in the lab. We both want this child to have the greatest chance of becoming Unbounded."

An Unbounded female's eggs couldn't be tampered with, but the Renegades had created several processes to alter a man's sperm, raising the likelihood of having an Unbounded offspring by twenty percent. Since I was descended from Ava, our chances of having an Unbounded child would be forty percent after genetic alteration, which was a lot better gamble than she'd had with Bronson, who had no Unbounded ancestry. Stella might not have to watch her child age and die while she remained young.

A smile curved her lips, though her eyes shone with tears. "No relationship?"

"What do you call this?" I moved a hand back and forth between us.

"You know what I mean."

She meant a physical relationship. Sex. I also knew that casual relationships weren't her standard, or something Renegade Unbounded condoned. Family to them was everything, and since all their physical relationships resulted in offspring, they were careful with their intimacy.

I wanted to tell Stella that I was hers. That I loved her like I never thought I could love anyone after Lorrie. That I would wait for as long as she needed. But I'd learned a thing or two in the past months about my Stella, my star. I had to make us something she would fight for, not something connected to a baby, not something she'd feel guilty about later. Besides, a declaration in this moment would forever link us to Bronson and his death, and I didn't want her to see me that way. Mortal. Even if I was.

I blew out a decidedly frustrated breath. "Let's give it a little time."

She nodded, her eyes holding mine. Something passed between us, unidentifiable yet powerful. As if she saw me—the real me—for the first time. I wasn't sure if that was good or bad.

"Okay," she said. "You've got yourself a deal."

Maybe she'd change her mind about both the baby and me once there was a little space between her and what had happened this week. That was okay because at least I'd know I hadn't taken advantage of the woman I loved. It was also possible that after time we could both move forward without the baggage of the past, baby or no.

Whatever happened, I didn't fool myself that it was going to be an easy road for either of us, but I didn't give up easily.

I might be the mortal brother in my family, but I was also a Renegade.

**THE END**

TEYLA BRANTON GREW UP AVIDLY READING SCIENCE FICTION AND fantasy and watching Star Trek reruns with her large family. They lived on a little farm where she loved to visit the solitary cow and collect (and juggle) the eggs, usually making it back to the house with most of them intact. On that same farm she once owned thirty-three gerbils and eighteen cats, not a good mix, as it turns out. Teyla always had her nose in a book and daydreamed about someday creating her own worlds.

Teyla is now married, mostly grown up, and has seven kids, including a three-year-old, so life at her house can be very interesting (and loud), but writing keeps her sane. She thrives on the energy and daily amusement offered by her children, the semi-ordered chaos giving her a constant source of writing material. Grabbing any snatch of free time from her hectic life, Teyla writes novels, often with a child on her lap. She warns her children that if they don't behave, they just might find themselves in her next book!

She's been known to wear pajamas all day when working on a deadline, and is often distracted enough to burn dinner. (Okay, pretty much 90% of the time.) A sign on her office door reads: DANGER. WRITER AT WORK. ENTER AT YOUR OWN RISK.

She loves writing fiction and traveling, and she hopes to write and travel a lot more. She also loves shooting guns, martial arts, and belly dancing. She has worked in the publishing business for over twenty years. Teyla also writes romance and suspense under the name Rachel Branton. For more information, please visit http://www.TeylaBranton.com.